LEOPOLD CHRIST

R. L. NAPOLITANO

Also by R.L. Napolitano

THE TWINS

GIRVAN

Dedicated to my sons Michael and Daniel. Without them there is no me.

Cover design by Christina Gedick

prologue

Moving through the cold and dark, a lone voyager continued on a journey begun so very long ago. There was no sense of destiny in this journey. There was no expectation of greatness or shadow of impending disgrace. There was no hint of importance. Just one of countless others lost in time and space, their eventual fate unknown.

Compared to the others, an absolute monster in size. Dangerous, deadly, powerful beyond all that could be imagined. A lethal, mindless menace to be feared by any unfortunate to cross paths. Contact would mean death. Instantaneous perhaps, or perhaps a slow demise, but regardless there would be no mercy. There could not be. It was only luck that had kept death away and luck was never meant to last forever.

The path taken had been predetermined ages ago and there was nothing to be done about it. If there was to be a fate during the journey, whether for glory or infamy, outside influence would need to be exerted to realize that fate. But the monster was patient. There was no urgency from passing time, nor desire for importance. If nothing happened that would be alright, too.

We travel through time, our existence of no concern except to a few. And then something happens. A chance encounter. A bump of bodies. A ripple of the air. And all that was before, is no longer. Fate has exerted its influence, and there is nothing to be done about it. We are powerless in its wake and we exist, or expire, at its whim

It had tumbled through the silent vastness of space for billions of years, a rock composed of ninety percent iron, an orphan left to wander alone. Set upon a predictable course that never allowed it to become part of something larger and grander, it continued on a lonely journey, hurtling along an elliptical path around the massive sun and traversing safely through a maze of planets and moons. While other rocks of lesser importance and girth had found sanctuary on these same planets and moons, the largest of them all still slowly tumbled unabated at thirty-one thousand miles per hour through the void.

The shape of the object was conical with bulbous ends and slightly more narrow in the middle. It tumbled like a gymnast, head over heels, and for such an immense object it seemed to do so with incredible grace. It neither gained nor lost speed in its journey, and the path it traveled never varied. A spot in space that it passed by would be revisited exactly twenty-seven years later. Thus it was and thus it had always been.

Six hundred and eighty-four miles of impressive length and two hundred and thirty miles at its greatest width, from a distance it appeared remarkably smooth from the layer of dust that covered it. The middle section of the asteroid had a thickness of ice that had formed over the layers of dirt. In the times when the beast was nearest to the sun, and the normal -73 degree Celsius temperature warmed, ice crystals would escape the surface giving the appearance of a comet. But this was no comet, no celestial object worthy of song and lore. It was not an object to be pointed to and marveled at as it sped by in a majestic display. No, not this monster. This gray dot in the universe was a grim reminder that all of life could be snuffed out at any time.

A million asteroids orbited this solar system, most spending their time between two massive planets whose gravitational pull kept them in rotation. Many were no larger than a hundred yards wide and most a lot smaller. Occasionally, when bumped, an asteroid would leave the rotation and go rocketing across the dark, alone, losing mass should it find itself in the grip of any large objects pull. If it lost enough mass it would burn up in a planet's atmosphere, a meteor racing to its demise. If not, it would impact into the moon or planet that attracted it and damage would depend on the size of the meteor still intact on impact. The impact of an object six hundred and eighty-four miles long by two hundred and thirty miles wide would be devastating to a planet. Totally devastating.

The beast, reaching the furthest point of its trajectory, became caught in the gravitational pull of the sun, pulling it back into the orbit it had traveled for two billion years. In mid tumble, the massive rock was powerfully impacted by another asteroid of much smaller size, crashing into it at twenty thousand miles per hour. The impact happened midway between the narrow ice covered section and the highest part of the tumbling rock. A crater over one hundred miles wide was blasted from the monster, sending thousands of smaller pieces of iron rock speeding across space to begin their own orbits, to search out their own destiny. As cataclysmic as the impact was, in the far reaches of the galaxy it was just one more collision in a universe that was created by such collisions, most of which were hundreds of times greater than it.

The massive asteroid, absorbing the impact, continued on its way as if nothing had happened. The tumbling motion was unaffected. The speed was still thirty-one thousand miles per hour. The silence as deafening as before. The trajectory of the asteroid, however, had been altered a half degree by the impact. Just a half degree. After two billion years, things were no longer predictable.

one

He lay on his side in the dark, his head resting on a bare arm, his thick hair and beard matted with sweat. After the tension of the hunt, and the blistering   heat of the day, the cool dirt felt pleasant on his skin. It had been a difficult hunt, the huge animal having put up a fierce fight, stomping and trumpeting, thrashing and charging, but in the end it had succumbed to the dozens of wounds they had inflicted on it. Two of the hunters had been hurt during the long, brutal attack, foolishly meeting the beast head-on instead of from the side, where it was safer, and smarter, to thrust with their sharp weapons. Both males were young, inexperienced, and foolish. It was always the young who took the greatest risks. It was their way of proving to the tribe that, when the time

6

came for new leadership, they would be the one who would lead. It was what he had done when he was young. He, too, had been reckless then.

In his exhausted sleep, he was having a dream of the hunt, his spear once again being the final thrust that punctured the beast's heart. It was then the noise awakened him. In his life, he had never heard such a noise. It was much louder than any bellow or roar from the many animals who roamed freely on the land around their home and who contested the tribe daily for mastery of the valley. It was more disturbing than the great flocks of birds who darkened the morning light, calling loudly to each other as they flew over the land in never ending swarms. It was more frightening than the terrible storms that ravaged the sky, the thundering, flashing anger causing the air to quiver and the trees to tremble. It did not stop and it was getting louder.

His eyes were now open, but in the darkness of the space he could not even see the rock wall that was just an arms reach away. He sensed that the noise meant danger, but that was just him being cautious. He was no longer young and reckless, the passing seasons of leading his people demanding him to be a wiser man, and it was wise to expect danger in everything he did not know or understand. It was caution that had kept him alive these many seasons. Yet, every time before, when he had sensed a danger, he would be on his feet, weapon in hand, prepared to battle if need be. Cautious, yet excited, by the expected danger. This night, however, he still lay on the ground, knees drawn up, heart pounding, eyes wide open, all because of a noise. He knew if he was awake, then so were the others.

They would be frightened. Like him, they would have no idea what was making the noise, only that it was new and that made it frightening. They would all be awake now, probably standing in the dark, mothers cradling the young, warriors reaching for their weapons, taking cautious backward steps, back into the depths of their spacious home. His back was to them as he lay there. But in the dark of the night, he would not have been able to see what they were doing even if he turned, and with the deafening noise he could not hear movement behind him, but he knew there was. And they would all be waiting for the same thing: him.

He was their leader. He was the biggest, the strongest, the wisest. After that last brutal battle with the dirty ones many seasons ago, he had led them to this place, a place of warmth and safety away from the mountain. Their bellies were full, their numbers grew, and they trusted him to keep them alive. This responsibility was what he had wanted when he was a young warrior, to be the leader, the decision maker, and while he was a harsh leader, he was fair, and no one in the tribe questioned his decisions. Now, they would be looking to him to fight against whatever was making the noise, and he could not show them that he was just as frightened as they were. Maybe even more frightened, because he would have to be the first to step out of their home.

There then came a brightness that made it seem like it was day, and the light that entered their home was brighter than daylight and he could now see the wall in front of him and the weapon that lay beside him. The light would also mean they could all see him, lying there, knees drawn up, looking weak and small. That, he could not allow. Quickly, he came to a sitting position and turned. He thought he would see them all standing way in the back, but they were all standing close to him. The females were rocking side to side while they held their babies, their faces showing the concern they always showed when the males were going on a hunt. The males, who always exhibited fierce stomping and excited grunting before a hunt, now stood motionless and he could see they were all frightened, for never had they seen such a light or heard such a noise. And still the noise was getting louder.

Coming quickly to his feet, he picked up his weapon and stood tall in front of his people. To him, death was preferable to weakness. Preferable to what had happened to the old man, too. Death was not to be feared. From the beasts of the valley, to the warring tribes that roamed the land, death was but a heartbeat away. And now there was this noise. After staring into the eyes of every male, making sure they understood he expected them to follow him outside, he lifted the stone pointed spear high, stomped the ground several times with a bravado he did not feel, pounded his fist on his chest and yelled his name, "Drak", several times. Turning, he walked to the opening and stepped out into the light. The others, carrying their spears, reluctantly followed.

Drak had only stepped a few paces into the night when he came to a stop, as did the others behind him. The females had all stepped out from their home, their curiosity overcoming their fear of the unknown. The entire group now stood at the opening, a few of them grunting, but mostly they stood in silence and wonder at what they saw.

Before them, the entire valley was lit as if it were morning, and in this false light they could see across the flat of the land, all the way to the wide, treacherous mountain a days walk away. It rose perilously from the valley like the head of the hairy, tusked beasts they hunted, broad and rounded with dangerous ridges. More rock than forest, it was difficult to climb, and with no animals upon it other than the horned sheep, they had no reason to journey back to their old dwelling.

Outside of their home the noise was even louder and it became painful to their ears. While the noise was all around them and could have been coming from anywhere, they saw where the light came from and they stood in wonder, not comprehending that such a beast existed, for high above their valley a huge bird flew, and from the belly of the beast an intense light shone.

In his curiosity of the creature, Drak was surprised to see that his heart was no longer pounding in his chest. The fear of the unknown was now gone, replaced with a strong desire to know more about this bird that could screech such a sound and turn night into day. He had never seen such a creature and he wondered at it. He knew not if it would be a deadly adversary, or if it was only flying across the sky on its way to somewhere else, beyond the valley, where other lands lay. Yet, even while he stood in awe, his brain was analyzing and plotting, looking for an advantage if it came down to a life or death battle against the creature.

There were no flapping wings that he could see from that distance like he had seen on the great birds that soared above the valley with such grace, spiraling ever lower in their search for food. Were he to have to battle such a bird, he had long ago decided, he would attempt to damage the wings, limit their ability to fly, keep them on the ground where he would have the advantage. But this beast had no wings that he could see.

What he could see, even from the distance of the mountain the creature was above, was that this bird was not moving and that confused him greatly. He had never seen a bird do that, just stay in one spot, motionless. He did not believe that was possible. But he knew there were lands beyond this valley, lands he had never seen, and he was wise enough to know that those lands may have many wondrous creatures in them and that one day those creatures could enter this valley. Were that to happen, he knew he would need to observe them, to learn, and to adapt. And so he watched.

And then, as suddenly as it had begun, the noise stopped, yet the valley did not become quiet again. There was a great deal of bellowing, roaring, trumpeting, as the animals of the valley were responding to the intrusion of their nightly rituals.

He sensed a relief in those behind him, but he felt no such calming. He understood that the ending of the terrifying noise would be the start of something else, perhaps even more frightening, and it did not take very long for that something else to begin. With a slowness that made one question if they were even seeing what they thought they were seeing, the bird began to drop from the sky, gently nearing the broad mountain top. Although it was difficult to see from that distance, it appeared the bird was also moving slowly towards them, eventually becoming larger as it neared, the harsh light that came from its belly growing brighter. Unlike other birds he had studied in their flight, birds that extended their wings and floated on the air, carried by a breeze, this bird flew straight, the wind having no effect on its path. The animals of the valley who had bravely roared against the noise, could now be heard running from the approaching bird, trampling across the valley as they rampaged towards the forest, seeking safety far from the valley. Whatever danger they had sensed, it was enough to send them into retreat. Drak noticed there was no grand exodus from the great flocks of birds that called the trees of the valley home, and he realized that they must have left the valley when the noise had started, sensing that there were safer places to roost.

When the tumult of the rampage was no more than fading echoes through the valley, all that was left was a faint humming in the air as the bird came ever closer to where the tribe stood by the entrance to their home. Behind him, Drak heard the whimpers of the females and the grunts of the males, and he sensed a great fear among them. He had no such fear, just an overwhelming sense of curiosity, because he no longer believed what he was looking at was a bird. He had no idea what it might be, but he did not believe it was a live creature. His limited imagination could not even begin to understand what it might be were it not alive, so his curiosity was even greater than his fear of danger.

Half way across the valley the bird stopped advancing and began to slowly lower toward a clearing of high grasses. While the grassed land below it was brightly lit, it was difficult to see the body of the massive bird that was as dark as the night time sky. As the bird settled even lower, the light became more concentrated under it and the tribe was once again standing in darkness, watching, the males expectantly ready, waiting for their leader to lead them forward in a dash to battle the beast.

The great bird settled on the ground and when it did light erupted from spots all around its massive body, once again sending harsh brightness across the valley and the tribe had to shield their eyes from the intensity of the light. Once again, noise erupted from the beast, and this time it was so loud they could feel the pain in their heads from the sound and they all wanted to flee back into their home. But the noise ended as quickly as it had started, and when it did they saw the belly of the beast begin to open up and once again their curiosity kept them where they stood.

In the intense light, they saw something come out from the belly of the bird, but they could not see what it was in the harshness of the light. Slowly, the bird began to rise from the ground, all the lights from around its body going dark with only the light from its belly still shining, and even that one was dimmed. But in that dimmed light, they saw two shapes standing beneath the bird as it rose and they were amazed. And frightened.

Drak looked at the two shapes, two shapes that looked like him, a male and a female, and he did not understand. What he did understand was, while they looked like him and his kind, they could not be the same, because he did not possess, nor had he ever seen, the kind of power that he had just witnessed. The male and female had come from within the belly of something that was certainly not a bird, but what it was he could not fathom.

The male and female stood in the clearing looking up to where the tribe silently stood and then they turned and began walking toward the mountain, the light leading the way. The tribe watched from their entrance, confused by what they had just seen and unsure as to what it all meant. Were they in danger? Drak did not think so. He had seen no weapons being carried by either of the two. No spear, no club. He saw no threat from them or from whatever had brought them to the valley. He watched them walking towards the mountain until he could no longer see them from that distance. He continued watching for a long time until, once again, the great bird settled over the mountain top, the light shining brightly over it. They all watched, scared and excited at the same time by what they were seeing, and still nervous about what the great bird would do next. Suddenly, the light from the beast went out and and it flew across the valley at a great speed, disappearing over the forest of trees, speeding toward a sky that was becoming light from a coming day. The valley became calm and quiet, and a morning fog began filling the space between their home and the mountain, eventually only the mountain top breaking through the haze. A mountain where only the horned sheep lived. Until now.

two

Many seasons had passed since the beast had opened its belly and left the man and woman behind. The flying creature had not returned, the noise had not again disturbed the valley, light had not again conquered darkness and the man and woman had not been seen again. If they still lived on the mountain, or had wandered into other lands, Drak had no way of knowing. He would not venture to the mountain, even though his curiosity about them was great. Two of the younger males had trekked to the mountain two seasons ago, but had seen nothing.

The valley had finally returned to the way things were before that night. The animals had come back to the valley to graze or hunt, assembled by the water to drink and the great flocks of birds again filled the trees. For several seasons after that disturbing night, beasts to hunt had been scarce in the valley and his people had survived by scavenging the remains of what other beasts left behind. But now they were hunting again and once more his people's bellies were full, the tribe growing larger and stronger.

It was early morning, the circle of light in the sky overcoming the chill of the night air. There would be no need for the animal skins on this day. He, and the other males, were preparing for another day of hunting, with some of the them using sharp rocks to make the points of their spears more deadly for the hunt. As Drak waited for them to make their preparations, he sat by his sleeping area, enjoying berries that the young ones had picked near the entrance to their home, and he watched the old man doing what the old man did most days now, dipping a clump of animal hair into a mixture of dirt, animal fat, animal blood and red ocher, and coloring in scratches the old man had made on the wall. Scratches that told the story of the tribes life. They showed the animals that lived in the valley, brave hunters in battle, life in their home. A short distance from where the old man now stood, a large section of rock depicted a memory of the great beast. The old man had made a large bird above two people with the great mountain in the distance. The old man had labored for many days on that, and when he had finished everyone could see that the old warrior had shown the night as they remembered.

Drak held a great affection for the old warrior who had once been the leader of the tribe, back when their home was nestled in the mountain many seasons past. As a reckless youth, Drak had sometimes questioned the old man's wisdom, and the old man always showed great patience in his youthful spirit. It was only after many years of being the leader, and the wisdom that comes with age and responsibility, that Drak now understood just how wise the old man had been. When the old man could no longer lead the tribe, Drak became the leader and he had brought them here, to this home, soon after that terrible day.

Most of the tribe's men had been on the hunt that cold day, moving along the base of the mountain, following the tusked beast that had been seen earlier that morning. Coming through dense forest into an open field on the far side of the valley, they were brutally attacked by another tribe of men who came charging at them from the forest, grunting loudly, swinging wooden clubs and lunging at them with sharp spears. The old man was a fearsome warrior that day, standing tall in the high grass, slaying many of the attackers, his spear red with their blood. It was a fierce battle they waged against the taller, wider men, and Drak remembered how excited he had been during the battle, expertly thrusting with his spear, lifting large rocks to crush the heads of the fallen. When the battle had turned against them, the attackers ran back into the woods in defeat, and there came much high pitched whooping and stomping by his tribe for their victory. There was a cost to the victory, however, as the tribe lost four males to death and three others to injury. The most serious injury was to the leader. Near the end of the battle, he had been stunned by a club to the side of the head that had driven him to a knee. Days later, he still could not rise from his sleep and Drak took over the leadership of the tribe, defeating Bre in a fight for superiority. Even now, many seasons since that battle with the warring tribe, the old man still had not recovered to be the warrior he once was, and he now spent his days in front of the wall.

With the preparations for the hunt complete, Drak

finished the berries and led his males toward the opening. As they passed by the old man, the old warrior looked up from his drawing and met the gaze of the man who had taken his responsibilities. Drak, looking into the old mans dull eyes, saw a great sadness there and he understood; when a man is born to be a warrior, life means very little when there are no battles left to fight. Long after the last man had left the entrance, the old man continued staring out to the valley, his face clouding over as if he were trying to remember something. Something that was important. But it would not come to him. Sighing, he then carefully dipped the animal hair into the sticky solution and touched it to the stone of the wall, creating a red, horned, hairy beast.

Twenty males journeyed down the long, winding path to the valley. Once there, Drak split the group into two. One group he sent toward the circle of light that was now above the dense forest to hunt for meat and hides for warmth. He led the others toward the open grassland that led toward the mountain, hoping to find the great tusked, hairy beast whose meat would feed the tribe for many days.

Crawling through the high grasses as they crested a

rise, they looked down to where animals in the valley often went for water. Three of the beasts they were searching for were there. With only ten males with him, he knew they could not defeat three of the massive beasts, so they would need to separate one from the others. Keeping low in the high grass they neared the water, and when close enough they charged at the three animals, whooping and stomping, maneuvering between the beasts who had turned to protect themselves. With patience and skill, the men prodded at the three beasts, deftly avoiding the sharp tusks that could cause instant death and the lethal swinging of the heavy trunk that could break bones. Slowly, their tactics turned the attention of two of the massive beasts away from the third. The animals trumpeted and roared, charged and retreated and charged again. Drak, and two others, baited the largest of the three beasts into moving away from the water's edge by feigning attacks and then retreating away from the animal's reactive charge, steadily falling further back into the tall grasses each time. While they were doing this, the other men were leading the other two beasts around to the far side of the water with prodding attacks and planned retreats, until, after a long battle, the hairy beasts were on the opposite side of the water from where they had been drinking, and, exhausted from the battle, retreated across the valley toward the safety of the forest.

The remaining beast now fought with a great fierceness, angrily attempting to gore the men, swinging his massive trunk in lethal arcs, stomping his thick legs whenever he got near an attacker. He had not yet made contact with any hunter, and that enraged him even more, so as the men fled further away from the water, the animal, choosing not to flee when given the chance, pressed the attack.

When the circle of light was high in the sky, the beast stood among the tall grass, now far from the water, breathing heavily, its massive head hanging low, the hairy body shuddering from the mighty exertion of the battle. The hunters stood a short distance away from the beast, leaning on their spears, resting, awaiting the arrival of the rest of their group who could be seen cresting the hill and running towards them. The exhausted animal could hear the men approaching and turned to eye them as they surrounded him.

Twisting around to see the enemy, and trumpeting his

anger at the attackers, the beast once again charged, but this time the hunters did not retreat. The men who were in the path of the charge did not fall further back, but instead moved to the side and in toward the others. After several charges, the beast found himself again in the middle of the circle of men, but the circle had become much smaller, and he was confused and breathing hard. And then, from different angles, the hunters began to attack him, their sharp spears prodding at his bulk, creating wounds, drawing blood.

The animal rose up on hind legs and crashed down at his attackers, trying to crush them under his bulk. His tired movements were slow, predictable. The hunters moved in, did their damage, and quickly stepped back, knowing one false step would lead to them being crushed. Drak kept pointing and grunting, giving directions to the men, pressing the attack.

Suddenly, the animal saw an opening in the circle of men, and his sense of survival overcame his anger and he charged through the attack, stuck by two more thrusts as he made his escape. Without hesitation, Drak began to run after the wounded animal, the others following after him, whooping, knowing they had the battle won and the beast could not last much longer. The kill was theirs. They could not allow the animal to die elsewhere only to be scavenged by the animals of the valley.

Exhausted and bloodied, the animal rampaged across the expanse toward the mountain, trumpeting angrily as he ran. Upon reaching the mountain, the beast plodded up the rocky incline that led to the rock strewn base of the summit, and there, trapped, turned to once again face his tormentors, his massive, bloodied body trembling from the exertion. He trumpeted loudly, the pitiful wail echoing across the valley.

The experienced hunters had separated, cutting off paths of retreat in each direction. With practiced patience, they closed in on the wounded animal, grunting loudly and stomping the ground, forcing the attention of the animal to swing back and forth, further confusing the beast.

He stood pawing at the ground, his back against the rock of the mountain, and awaited the first hunters charge. It came from in front of him. One of the men, his spear thrusting, charged at the animal, but came to a stop when the beast rose up to meet the challenge. And then from the

27

side, the hairy beast was stuck by another hunter, once again drawing blood. Swinging his body to confront that attacker, the beast was stabbed from the other direction, and that hunter quickly retreated to safety. Turning to confront the second attacker, the beast smartly continued all the way around rather than stopping in its spin, and met the attack of another hunter who was expecting the animal to be facing away from him. The animal's trunk pounded into the attacker, sending him sprawling to the ground, and before he could crawl to safety the mighty beast reared up and crushed his weight down on the unfortunate man. The animal then trumpeted loudly, finding renewed energy with the kill.

The other hunters hesitated for just a moment, the death of one of them raising a fear in them. Then one of the younger males charged angrily at the animal, his spear aiming for the eyes of the beast. But the beast was too quick, his tusk deflecting the spear and his trunk bashing into the man sending him against the stone of the mountain. Stunned by the power of the beast, he could not react quick enough as the animal lowered his head and gored him, almost ripping him apart.

While the hunters were absorbing this second death and the sudden turn in the battle, they had not noticed that the two beasts they had chased into the forest were now charging into the battle, their loud trumpeting announcing their arrival. As the hunters turned to face the charge, the larger of the two animals gored a hunter, raising him off the ground before violently flinging him away.

The hunters now found themselves in a battle for their lives and there was much confusion among them. Most of them fled to the base of the mountain, knowing that if they could climb up into the rocks they would be safe. The beasts pressed the attack now, chasing the men, trying to gore and stomp on them as they moved up the rocky incline. Two more men were battered before reaching the safety of the rocks.

Watching the battle from atop a large rock, an angry Drak leaped upon the back of the wounded, bloodied beast and repeatedly drove his spear into the animal, causing massive wounds. The animal, near death, found the strength to rear up once again and that sent his tormentor crashing to the ground. Dazed, Drak looked up at the animal who

29

towered over him panting heavily. Slowly, the animal's front legs bent and he collapsed onto his knees in front of his tormentor, his black eyes staring at the fallen warrior. Hunter and hunted stared at each other as the battle raged all around them. Then, with a great effort, the beast struggled to a standing position, once again towering over the prone man. Raising his head, he trumpeted one last time, then reared up, prepared to crush the hunter under his bulk.

Awaiting his death, Drak, still dazed from the impact of the fall, saw a bolt of light explode through the beast, knocking the animal backwards and destroying most of the huge head. A thunderous noise echoed across the valley. No sooner had the echo died, when he saw another blaze of light flash off the mountain, killing another of the beasts. This light was also followed by the thunderous noise.

As Drak struggled to his feet, amazed to still be alive, he watched the third beast fleeing across the field towards the forest. Confused, Drak picked up his spear, marveled at the dead creature before him, then moved away from the side of the mountain, looking for those who had survived the battle. Beside the body of the second beast, five of his men, leaning on their spears, stood looking up at the mountain. As Drak walked up to them, he looked to see what they were looking at. There, standing above them, and not very far away, were a male and a female. Their bodies were covered, but not by animal skins. The female held a baby in her arms. Beside the male stood a small boy. The male held a shiny object in his hand that was not much larger than the hand that held it. They stood motionless, staring down at the hunters.

Drak realized these must be the two who had come from the bird's belly. They now had young ones. He saw that they looked like him, but there were differences. Their bodies were thinner, less muscular, and much taller. Their faces were thinner, more narrow, smoother. They stood more erect. The woman's hair was light in color, the man's face hairless.

More importantly, he knew, their weapon was much more powerful than his weapons. While it took many thrusts from his weapon to down a creature, their weapon could destroy any beast with just one thrust.

They stood staring at each other, Drak unsure if they were in danger. Then the tall man raised his hand with the shiny object in it and pointed it at the remaining hunters. The others began grunting nervously and taking backward steps, but their leader stood still and looked up at the man. He had seen what that shiny object could do, but he was not afraid. It had saved his life and the lives of the others.

Dropping his spear on the ground, Drak dropped to his knees, spread his arms out wide and bowed his head. He heard much grunting behind him, and when he looked all the others had done the same. He then looked up to the man and woman on the mountain. The man stared down at them, then slowly lowered his hand with the shiny object that shot bolts of light, turned and began walking up a path, the woman following, until they were out of sight.

three

"Doctor Reynolds, we have found something," Madeline said excitedly as she entered the tent. "You need to see it."

I was sitting at the foldaway table making exact documentation of the articles we had found the past few days, logging dates, times, matching items to numbered spots of discovery. There were over two hundred artifacts and it was a time consuming business. We needed to be out of there in the next few days, so I really didn't have time for the exuberant young Madeline who treated every discovery of another pointed piece of rock as the finding of the Holy Grail. Oh, to be that young and that exuberant again.

"What have we found this time, Madeline?" I asked, a playfulness in my voice as I kept scribbling into my notebook. Madeline was one of eight college students selected to assist me on this dig from a list of twenty-seven who had applied. Over the six weeks, I had found her to be brilliant and, more importantly, extremely passionate about what we were doing. She would, I believe, someday make a name for herself in archaeology.

"Have we found a spearhead that is different from the ones in front of me?" I asked. I could be a sarcastic son-of-a-bitch at times when people pissed me off. I sometimes found myself doing it to people who didn't upset me, too. I may have developed the technique at a young age when dealing with all the people who kept asking why I couldn't be more like my older brother. Of course, the tone of my voice was quite different depending on the situation. This time, I was having fun. "Perhaps another fragment of bone, only this one is larger than the finger bones I have on this table. Did someone find another painting on the wall that we missed? Perhaps to rival the great Masters?"

Placing the pen down and turning toward my young assistant, I said, "Wait, don't tell me. You have found the Ark of the Covenant, buried in this cave centuries ago by the

Knights Templar."

"Doctor Reynolds..."

"No, no, let me guess. I can see by the excitement in your eyes that this is big. I have it. You have found the missing link. You, Madeline DeBarge, have found the missing link in a cave in France. You must excuse me now, my young colleague, I need to alert the scientific community. Discoveries this big must not be kept secret."

"Are you done, Doctor?" Madeline said, her voice informing me she did not find my playful banter cute this time.

I smiled. "Yes, Madeline, I am done. I really am quite busy with this documentation," I said, waving my hand at the artifacts on the table. "Does this really require my attention?"

Once again her eyes lit up and it was obvious she was quite excited and that excitement had not been tempered by my attitude toward her announcement.

"Doctor, you really need to see this."

I sighed, then smiled at the tall, thin woman from the University of Milan who had actually grown up just over a hundred miles from where we now were.

I tried one more time, even while I was coming to my feet. "Can't you tell me what it is you found, Madeline? Must I trek up that path again today? I'm not as young as I used to be, young lady."

She reached out and grabbed at my hand, her eyes radiant, and began pulling me to the opening of the large white tent. "This will make you feel young again, Doctor. You'll see."

We stepped out into the warmth of the day, the sun very near its apex in a brilliant blue sky. A half dozen tents ran along the path to the base of a mountain, and then the path ran on a steep angle up the mountain side. On both sides of the gravel path there were row after row of productive grape vines, their fruit soaking up the heat of the sun, growing fat and full of juice so that one day soon they could be picked and then pressed into dry, red Bordeaux wine. From this level, only the long rows of the vineyard could be seen. But from the level of the cave we were walking to, fifty-five meters above us, the vineyard's chateau was visible, a long, sprawling structure that was begun in the early 1700's and had been owned by the same family ever since. Three hundred years is, I am sure, quite old to most people. However, when you are digging up things that are maybe 50,000 years old, three hundred years really is nothing more than a second in time.

The mountain probably should not have been designated a mountain, because a mountain conjures up images of Everest or Kilimanjaro, and this piece of rock certainly hadn't attained such lofty heights. It barely stood three hundred meters above the valley that it divided, but it so dominated the immediate landscape that mountain did seem an apt designation for the lone, ugly nodule that marred the beauty of the rest of the land. On the other side of the mountain, two other century old chateaus were home to magnificent vineyards that ran all the way across the valley to the hills. Near the base of those hills, a large section of land had been excavated forty years before, when the bone of a mammoth had been unearthed by one of the vineyards expansions. That site was still worked periodically over the years when more funding could be attained. It had proven to be a valuable site in terms of understanding the animals that had called the valley home in the prehistoric past. Beyond the valley was the town, that was very near the size of a city, that prospered along the Vezere River.

Walking beyond the tents, there was an open area where the students played aggressive volleyball contests most nights after dining. It was here the vans were parked, waiting to be loaded up tomorrow with all of our belongings. Most people, I would imagine, would be surprised at how much stuff eight young people think they need for a six week dig. I have learned over the years to travel light, taking along only the most basic needs. College students, however, seem to think they need to bring their entire dorm room with them. It is strange indeed, that a twenty year old can trek across Europe on foot or bike all summer long with all they need in a backpack, yet when they don't have to actually carry things there is a ton of stuff they can't be without. I find I need a sense of humor when dealing with young adults.

Climbing up the steep incline, I felt my knees creaking. I hadn't been fooling when I had said to Madeline that I wasn't as young as I used to be. All these years of kneeling on dirt and rock, climbing mountains and ladders, sleeping on cots too small for my height, had done a number on my knees. I think I know what running backs in the NFL feel like when they finally hang up the cleats. I'm only forty-six years old, but I move like a man thirty years older.

"Come on, Doctor, you have to see this," Madeline said again, as she paused and turned back to see me fifty feet behind her.

"After six weeks of trekking up this path, Madeline, I am pretty sure I know my way. The knees are going, young lady, not the mind." And then, "This better be good or I'm leaving you here tomorrow."

Madeline just gave me a disgusted look, having absolutely no sympathy for my infirmity, then turned and bounded up the path on long, lean, young legs. Damn her.

Upon reaching the entrance to the cave, I looked out over the expanse of the valley. It was a view I never tired of. I could imagine myself stepping out of the cave in the early morning, a warm sun burning off the fog, revealing a land where huge bears fearlessly walked across fields of tall grasses, woolly mammoths plodded along the edge of forests, saber-toothed tigers skulked in the grass near water awaiting an opportunity to pounce upon unsuspecting deer. A valley teeming with wild life millenniums ago, millenniums after the ice had receded.

This was not my first time to these valleys. Twenty-five years before, I had been a college assistant on a dig in a cave across the valley on the opposite side of this mountain, directly above the excavation of the mammoth pit. I had returned to that dig for three consecutive years while I was working on my doctorate and I learned a lot from the old professor from the University of Munich who was in charge of the dig. That cave, along with the mammoth pit excavation, had unearthed a treasure trove of valuable artifacts that laid out the history of this section of Europe throughout the last fifty thousand years. The cave I was now excavating had not yet been that rewarding, which I thought to be confusing, but I would come back a second time in a few years when I got enough funding and dig a little deeper.

"Okay, Madeline, what have we got?" I said as I entered the cave and slowly limped over to where she stood.

"Oh, bueno, Professore, you are here," Esteban said from the base of the excavation two and a half meters below me.

"It's Doctor, Esteban," Madeline yelled down at him, but he ignored her. When Madeline wasn't around he called me Doctore.

"Come down the ladder, Professore. You need to see this."

The last thing my poor knees wanted to do was climb down a ladder, but Esteban was down there dusting dirt away from something and maybe it would be a fragment of a skull or mandible that had belonged to a Neanderthal and wouldn't that be marvelous. That would get me easy funding for another dig the following summer.

Half way down the ladder, Esteban raised his hand towards me and said, "Stop!"

"What's the problem?" I asked, standing with both feet on the same rung and looking down at him.

He was on his feet now, his head coming to the level of my feet. He said, "Turn slowly, Professore, and look at the wall behind Madeline."

"What is this, Esteban?" I said. "We don't have time for games. You know that. You two were supposed to be

41

packing this place up."

"It's no game, Doctor Reynolds," Madeline said and there was a smile playing upon her lips. "Now look at my knees."

Looking up at her face, I frowned.

"My knees, Doctor. My knees."

So I looked at her knees and said, "You could be Olive Oyl's twin."

"Who?"

"Never mind," I said, looking back up to her face that now looked confused. "Madeline, what are we doing here?"

"Keep looking at her knees," Esteban then said, "and when she moves away keep looking straight ahead."

Looking down at the senior from the University of Madrid, I gave him my best frown, then returned my gaze to the knees of Madeline. She moved out of my line of sight and now I was staring at the limestone wall of the cave.

"Okay, now what?"

"Keep staring at the wall, Doctore," Esteban whispered. "Relax, and just keep your eyes on the lower part of the wall. And relax."

Seconds ticked by and I kept staring at the cold dark brown stone, trying to see what Esteban and Madeline wanted me, expected me, to see, but I wasn't seeing it. There were no painted images that we had missed. There was nothing. But then, just as I was about to proclaim I was seeing nothing, I saw it. I could scarcely believe what I was seeing, but I saw it.

When the shock wore off, I said, "It's not possible. I mean, I see it. But it's not possible."

Madeline did a little dance and spun around, clapping her hands together like a child.

"What do you think it is, Doctor?" she asked.

"I have no idea," I said as I climbed back up the ladder, Esteban following. "It may be nothing, but I believe it has to be something."

I walked slowly over to the section of wall that I had been staring at, approaching it as one might a cobra. Kneeling, I ran my hands over the rock, affirming with my sense of touch what my sense of sight had seen. Even then, I questioned the evidence. My fingers ran horizontally along a straight line for about five feet, feeling a minute crease in the wall that was perfectly level. At the end of each part of the line, I could trace another minuscule aperture vertically down to the floor of the cave. The entire rectangle was approximately sixteen inches above the floor. When I satisfied myself that these lines were in fact cuts in the stone, I sat down on the floor of the cave and gathered my thoughts. My two assistants stood behind me.

"Who discovered this?" I asked.

"I did, Doctor," Esteban whispered. "Quite by accident. I stopped on the way down the ladder, just where you had stood, adjusting my earphones, casually looking around, and there it was. I didn't know what to make of it. I thought I was seeing things. Then I called Madeline to come and look. She spotted it right away."

"Right away, Doctor," Madeline interrupted. "I can't believe I hadn't noticed it before. I've been up and down this ladder a hundred times. Of course, I'm always looking the other way, but....."

I leaned forward and scraped away a few inches of dirt and saw that the line continued its' vertical run below ground level.

"I know school starts in a week, and I'm sure you both have a lot to do, so if you can't stay I'll...."

"I'm not going anywhere, Professore," Esteban interrupted. "Not now."

"School can wait, Doctor Reynolds," Madeline said, sitting down beside me in the dirt, hugging her knees and staring at the wall. "And when the others see this, they'll all stay."

"What do you think it could be?" Esteban asked, taking a seat beside Madeline.

Shaking my head, I whispered, "I can't be certain. If it is from the same time period as the other things we have found in this cave, well, no one has ever come across anything like it. It would be incredible. Truly incredible."

^   ^

I called my university and told them the news and that I may not be there when classes began. The dean wished me luck and said they could manage for a while if need be. Six of the students stayed and we got busy the very next day. The first thing we needed to do was dig out the floor of the cave the width of the horizontal aperture until we reached the base of the vertical lines. This had to be done carefully, like any dig would be done. Most of what we were digging after the first thin layer of dirt was bat dung and animal waste that had accumulated in the cave over thousands of years. We ended up digging down over half a meter before reaching the point where the vertical lines ended. Scrapping carefully in the rock, we removed sediment that had filled another perfect horizontal line along the base. When all the paper thin spaces were scrapped, and all sediment removed, I stood looking at a three foot high by five foot wide rectangle that was perfectly etched into the stone of the wall, with lines that were amazingly smooth. It was the most incredible thing I had ever seen and it was my hope that it held the promise of something even more incredible.

In the area we had excavated during our six weeks in the cave, which was directly across from the rectangle, we had come across some animal bones and evidence of animal life in the cave a half meter below the current level, giving us a history of thousands of years that the cave had been used by animal life in the valley. Two meters below the current level, we had found evidence of man living in the cave; spear heads of stone, primitive tools, and two fragments of bone which I believed, when analyzed, would be from Cro Magnon humans, who, of course, are us. Years ago, when I had assisted in the cave across the valley, above the mammoth graveyard, we had unearthed bone fragments also, and they had been carbon dated to about twelve thousand years before, and were designated Early European Modern, or the more widely used term Cro Magnon. At almost three meters down in that cave, we had also found bone fragments from a jaw and several teeth. Those had been carbon dated to almost fifty thousand years and were Neanderthal. Neanderthal being the designation for a species of hominoid that had first been discovered in a cave near Neander, Germany a hundred years before. It had been my hope to find more evidence of Neanderthal in this cave, but we had found none.

"What is the plan, Professore," Esteban asked as we sat in a tight circle around a campfire in front of the tents, resting from a long day of excavating.

All eyes were on me. There had been a lot of excitement the past few days and a lot of wild speculations about what we may have found, but the reality was we had no idea if we had really found anything.

"Well," I began, "we really don't know what we have, do we? It may be nothing."

"How can that be, Doctor Reynolds?" Madeline asked. "Those lines are absolutely perfect and appear to be very deep. How could that have been done thousands of years ago and by who? And why?"

"Let's not forget that huge stone blocks were being cut thousands of years ago for the pyramids," I said while staring into the fire and trying to be very careful in the words I used and the tone of my voice. "Who really knows how old Easter Island is. Or Stonehenge."

"But there isn't one chip on either side of those lines, Doctor Reynolds," Clay Hunt said. Clay is one of my students from the university and would be entering his senior year when we got back. "There isn't a mark, a scratch, any indication that tools had been used to make that slit. How is that possible?"

"I don't know," I said. "Look, it is very probable that these slits in the rock are no more than that. How they were made, I don't know. But here is what I am hoping it is, and if I am right then this will be a major discovery. What archaeologists know is that Cro Magnon, early man, buried their dead. Some have even suggested that they held some kind of a rite for the occasion. Now, there is no evidence that a casket of some kind was used. It was just putting the body into a hole in the ground, but it was a significant step up from what earlier hominoids did with their dead."

I paused, not sure I wanted to divulge my thoughts. If I was wrong, and more than likely I was, it wouldn't take long for my wild idea to race throughout the archaeological community and everyone would have a good laugh at my expense. It is never a good thing in my field when that happens. One success can give a man years of notoriety, and a great success immortality. One hint of folly can follow a man to his grave. We all talk a good game when we praise the success of others, but we are a jealous lot and despise the fact it wasn't us who found those bones, and we can be quite an unforgiving society when one of us is shown to be a fool. I needed to be very careful.

"What we are going to do tomorrow, now that the base

49

is ready, is drill six holes into the rock wall inside the etched lines. One in each of the four corners of the rectangle and two in the middle of the rectangle about a foot apart. We will then cement eye hooks into those holes with fast bonding adhesive. Then we wait twenty-four hours."

It was Clay who spoke first. "Are you saying you think that may be some kind of a burial chamber inserted in the wall, Doctor Reynolds? A perfectly cut sarcophagus that has been inserted into a perfectly cut hole with no tolerance what-so-ever by people who lived maybe ten thousand years ago? How could that be possible with the crude tools they possessed?"

Once again, all eyes looked at me.

I had to smile. That was exactly what I was saying, only I couldn't say it. "I think what we need to do is eliminate one thing before we consider something else that we could then prepare to eliminate," is what I did say.

"Look, we will insert the hooks, attach some rope to them, and then pull. If the rectangle part of that wall begins to pull away from the wall itself, well then, we have something pretty spectacular, right? If we can't budge it, then

50

we can decide if we want to drill larger holes into the wall and see if there may be a space back there. If that proves uneventful, we will all go back to our schools and I will spend this winter contemplating all kinds of crazy things that will have me quite pumped up when I come back here in a year or two. At the very least, it may help me get the funding I will need."

"But you think it is a burial chamber, don't you Doctor?" Madeline asked as she looked at me from the other side of the fire. "Who could have put it there? Could such a thing be possible?"

"I don't know. I don't know. And I don't know. I'm afraid, Madeline, that is how I have to answer your questions. But in two days, we may have some answers. Until then, I have some documentation I need to finish up." Standing, I left them with a final thought. "So I leave you all to ponder the great unknown. Remember, we can hypothesize all we want, but the only thing that matters is results. Proven and tested. And then tested again. We leave conjecture to the fiction writers of the world. Science is based on facts. Proven and tested. Good night." I waved to them and headed for my tent.

It would be a lie if I said I wasn't excited. I do believe that is some kind of a burial tomb inserted into the wall. If it is, and carbon dated to stone age time over ten thousand years before, it would change everything. A chamber like that could only mean the body inside was one of great importance to whoever put it there. There was no documentation of anything like this being done by a tribe or society until thousands of years later. None. And how could it possibly have even been done with the crude tools we know they had then. Or at least the ones we know they had. In less than forty-eight hours, I would have some answers.

^   ^

Clay and I had the middle ropes. Esteban and Madeline on our left, Ian and Gretchen on our right. I could feel the excitement in the group. Sam had done her best in spraying a lubricant into the thin slits. Hopefully, it would help. I had no idea how heavy the rectangular box would be, if indeed it was a burial chamber, or even the depth of it. If it was too large, we would need equipment to move it. Equipment we didn't have, or could easily get. That would mean a winter of wondering.

"On three pull. Pull with everything you have. Ready? One, two, three."

The ropes went taut and the students and I groaned in our exertion. Feet dug into the dirt, muscles bulged, one or two curses escaped young lips, and it felt like we were tugging on an Abrams Tank. The results were not good.

"Okay, ease up," I said after a minute, letting go of the rope.

"We can do this, Professore," Esteban said. "I could feel it ready to move. Another second or two, a bit more muscle, and it would have come."

"Sure, if the muscle was Hercules," said Ian. "I didn't feel we were getting anywhere, Doctor, what if we used some come-alongs? We could attach three of them to the opposite wall and crank."

"I thought of that, Ian, but we don't have any with us and it would take some time to get them and set them up." I then addressed the group. "Look, this little project is already eating into the time you need to be getting to your classes. The cave isn't going anywhere. It will be here next year, and

53

I'll come back with the right equipment and give it another go. And I'll invite you all back."

"Are you giving up, Doctor Reynolds?" came the taunt from Madeline. "I agree with Esteban. That section of wall felt ready to move. I say we give it a few more tries."

"Let's do this," said Clay.

I smiled and shook my head a little at the spirit of the young. I had the feeling that we were pulling on a whole mountain and not something inserted into it. But the passion of youth must be served.

"Fine. Another try. But let's move some people around first. Clay and Esteban, take the bottom ropes. Madeline, Gretchen and Sam take these middle ropes. Ian and I on the top ropes. On three we give it all we got."

When everyone was in place and ready, I did the countdown and we all strained at the ropes. There was much grunting, a little swearing, and pleas to keep pulling. Finally, I yelled, "Stop."

Taking a sitting position, and deep breaths, I said, "We're getting nowhere. Look we will drill into the wall as far as we can and see if we hit something hollow. It is probable that those lines are nothing more than that. Just etched lines. No idea why, or how they got there, but just lines."

"Professore," said Esteban, running his hand along the wall. "It moved."

"What?" I said, coming to my feet.

"The wall. She has moved. Just a little, but I can feel it. It is no longer smooth along the lines."

I ran my hands over the etched lines. Esteban was right. It was no longer smooth. Maybe an eighth of an inch. Maybe a quarter of an inch. But we had moved it.

"Everyone grab the ropes again," I said, not concealing my excitement. "Same places. On three pull like crazy."

After a half hour of effort, Clay and Esteban went for more water while the rest of us sat and rested weary muscles and sore hands. The rectangle was now jutting two inches into the cave. If there was a carved out section where bones, or whatever, had been placed, we still could not see into it, but we could now see that this wasn't just a section of a one dimensional wall. This was, in fact, some kind of a container. The first inch out of the wall had been painfully

55

slow, the second a little easier.

"What do you think is in there, Doctor Reynolds?" Madeline asked as she sat beside me flexing sore fingers.

"Well, my young friend," I said, "my first inclination is there is a body. Even though no one has ever discovered any evidence of early man doing anything like this. Of course, it could me a tomb filled with things early man may have considered quite valuable. Either way, whatever it is, Madeline, it will be amazing."

"You know, Doctor, my friends say to me all the time, Madeline, they say, why do you want to spend your life digging in the dirt? What is wrong with you? You are a pretty girl. Find a rich man. Live the easy life. Wiggle your painted toes in the sands of Monte Carlo instead of the dirt of a filthy cave."

"And what do you say to them, Madeline?"

"I just smile at them, Doctor. They could never understand this. They could never feel what I am feeling right now. The excitement. My whole body is tingling even in its exhaustion and pain. This must be what it feels like to conquer the highest mountains." She looked at me. "Did you have such feelings on your first important digs? When you found those bones across the valley?"

I smiled at her and took one of her cramped hands into mine and massaged the palm of it. "Yes, I did. And I have them now, too. Digging and searching for ancient things, and teaching others how to do it, has been my life for many years. Most people couldn't possibly understand what we do. You will never regret not wiggling your toes into the warm sands of a beach, because there will be other incredible memories that will warm you in the quiet of the night."

"What made you decide on taking archaeology in school, Doctor? Were you fascinated with dinosaurs as a boy growing up? I know with me, my fascination began with a trip to a museum when I was twelve and saw the display of early man confronted by a saber-toothed tiger. Those massive canine teeth. I was hooked."

Feeling the knot loosen, I released her hand. "There really was no fascination with any one thing," I said to her. "I think, in my situation, it was a conscious decision brought on by the simple facts of my life at that time. Simply put, I was never going to measure up to my brother. By the time he

57

graduated college, it was apparent to everyone who knew Matthew Reynolds, that he was going places. He had a chance, in the years to come, to be a force in the future of our state and maybe even the country. I was in high school at the time, pretty much a confused kid about almost everything, and I knew I would always be his younger brother, living in the shadow. I guess I decided if he was the future then I would go in another direction. While he searches for solutions to lead the country forward, I search for answers from the past. I've never regretted that decision."

We labored until lunch, having slipped the rock forward another inch. After a light lunch, we again took our places on the ropes and put our tired muscles to work. Slowly, we brought it out another inch.

"Doctor Reynolds," Clay said as we relaxed our grip on the ropes to rest once again. I looked over at him and he had a huge smile on his face. Going to where he stood, I saw that we had cleared the rim of the rectangle and there was a space. I grabbed a flashlight and shone light down into that void. I could not make out anything in that narrow aperture except that this was indeed a container of some kind and it did contain something.

There was a great adrenaline rush at that point from everyone and we all grabbed up the ropes one more time. It appeared that once the rim of the container had cleared the wall it became much easier to pull and the bulk of the thing slid out revealing the entire open area of the box. They all stood around it as I pointed the light into the container. There was a four inch rim all the way around the perimeter of the container that was highly polished and smooth as glass, as was the interior. A hide of some kind of an animal, it appeared to be deer, stretched over whatever was on the bottom of the container. I lifted it gingerly and pulled it back towards me.

"Oh, my, God!" I heard Madeline say.

four

"Doctor Reynolds?"

Looking up from the paper I was reading, I saw an elderly man standing at the open door to my small office at the university. He was wearing a perfectly tailored dark brown wool suit, white dress shirt and light brown tie. His thinning gray hair was cut short. He was short of stature and sickly thin. He held an elaborately carved cane in his right hand, but he stood erect so it hardly appeared it was needed. The skin of his face was ashen gray and pulled tight against the bones, almost disturbingly so. The face almost a mask of a skull. Lips were thin. If you picture old photographs of the elderly John D. Rockefeller you will have an idea of the man who stood at my door. The most amazing thing about the old gentleman, however, were the eyes. They seemed to blaze an intensity that was noticeable even from where I sat.

"Yes," I said, standing to greet him. "And you must be Mr. Chase. Please come in."

Coming around the desk to greet the man and to clear off a chair so he could sit, I offered a handshake. Instead of shaking my hand, he placed a business card into it.

"I'm afraid Mr. Chase will not be joining us," he said as he glanced around the clutter of the office. "He is an acquaintance of mine, Doctor, but is not needed here."

It was a plain bone white card with only a name printed in the center of it. *Leopold Christ.*

"I'm afraid I don't understand, Mr. Christ. I thought I was meeting with the curator of the Chicago Museum."

He stood looking at the power wall by the side of the desk. Like everyone else who recently glanced over the wall, the frames that held my scholarly accomplishments were quickly scanned while the photos with my more famous older brother were lingered on.

"Yes," he said, his voice barely above a whisper. "A

common mistake."

"I'm sorry," I said, a bit confused. "What mistake might that be?"

He turned from the wall and fixed his eyes upon me. A hint of a smile creasing those thin lips. "My name, of course, Doctor. You pronounced it Christ, as in Jesus Christ. That is not how it is pronounced. It is Christ, as in rhymes with list. Leopold Christ, sir." And he gave a slight bow of the head.

I awkwardly returned the bow. "I apologize, Mr. Christ."

"No need for that," he said, giving a slight dismissive wave of his free hand. "As I said, a common mistake. I probably should have chosen something different, but we all learn from our mistakes, don't we, Doctor? Nothing to be done about it now." He looked back at the pictures on the wall. "What about you, Doctor Daniel Arthur Reynolds? Are you happy with your name?"

I shrugged. "It is what my parents chose. They didn't ask my opinion."

"Perhaps," he said as he moved across the room with short, quick steps to read the titles of the books I had on two shelves on the wall, "if your parents had decided to call you Matthew and your brother Daniel, your office would be much larger and his this small."

Taking my seat once more behind my cluttered desk, I said, "Our names don't define us, Mr. Christ, our actions do." I had had enough nonsense talk. "As you can imagine, sir, I am quite busy. I have another class in an hour. What can I do for you and why was I told I was meeting Mr. Chase?"

He took the chair I had cleaned off opposite me and leaned forward with both hands on his cane, fixing me with those intense eyes. "It is the trouble with the world today, Doctor Reynolds. Everyone is always so busy. They have no time for conversation. No time for a new acquaintance to learn something about them. In days gone past, two men would sit on comfortable over-stuffed chairs and chat over fine brandy, speaking of nothing very important. Yet, in that idle conversation, they could take the measure of the other, and in that measure decisions could be made. Was the man someone who could be trusted? Was he honorable? Did he have fortitude? Was he frivolous, or a man of substance? All these things an intelligent man could discern of another

63

during an evenings discourse. Now, in these new and disturbing times of the computer age, when someone wants to know about someone else, they Google them and think they know all there is to know about that person. A list of wonderful accomplishments for all to see, along with the less desirable happenstances that may have befallen the individual. And on the basis of those few words that blast about the internet like electrons in the atom, are important decisions made. Unfortunate, I believe."

"And if I was to Google Leopold Christ, what accomplishments, great or ill, would I be reading?" I asked.

Again that slight parting of thin lips. "You will find nothing, my dear Doctor. There is no accomplishment that I attach my name to. No marvelous composition of words or mastery of paint or rock have I attained. No earth shattering addition to science or medicine can be attributed to me. I am a very old man who has never sought notoriety. As far as I know, there are no photographs of me. I have few acquaintances and fewer friends."

Leaning back in my desk chair, I said, "A man of mystery then. I do not recall ever hearing your name or reading anything in the newspapers or on line about anyone named Leopold Christ. Yet, you, sir, managed to get the very well known and respected Clive Chase to misrepresent a meeting with me. That suggests to me that you are someone." I smiled. "You do realize, that I could take out my phone, call my brother, and he could have any information on you within minutes."

"Even faster than that, Doctor Reynolds. Your brother knows of me, although we have yet to meet. And that is something, that in the very near future, we shall correct."

I looked at this old man with the intense eyes in the barely concealed skull, and felt a slight shiver shake my body, almost like a premonition of doom surrounded him. Silly, really, and the feeling was gone in a moment.

"What can I do for you, Mr. Christ? Can I call you Leopold? Or Leo?"

"I think not, Doctor Reynolds," he said, a frown upon his face that did not quite look as horrible as the smile did upon that countenance. "And it is not what you can do for me, Doctor, at least not initially, but more what I can do for you."

65

"You can do something for me?" I said, raising my eyebrows and smiling. I had no idea what he was talking about. "Please explain."

"Obviously," he said, "this has to do with your find in France several months ago."

"Well, not so obviously," I replied, "because I don't see where it could possibly concern you, but it does seem to be what everyone wants to talk about. How does my find concern you, sir, and how much do you know about it?"

"I know enough. Have the results come back yet?"

"Preliminary only. Final results should be back later this month."

"I see. And what do you think, Doctor, those results will tell us?"

" I would rather not speculate. We will know soon enough."

"But you have definite thoughts, Doctor. You must. A man with your experience...."

"A man with my experience," I said, interrupting him, "doesn't talk about his thoughts. He waits for the facts and then lets the facts do the talking."

The old man nodded his head several times. "My dear Doctor, this conversation will never be known beyond these cluttered walls. I only ask for your instinctive intuition on what you found. What did those old bones tell you?"

I sat silent for quite a long time, looking around the room and occasionally at the old man who knew about the bones that had been in the sarcophagus, wondering just how much he did know, and how much I would tell someone I didn't personally know.

"What is it you want?" I finally asked. "Were you an amateur archaeologist in your younger days? Are you some kind of religious zealot who believes we have found the bones of the man whose name doesn't rhyme with list? Some kind of fanatic, looking to debunk scientific evidence that has been unearthed over the past two hundred years? What's your interest in all of this?"

He fixed me with that penetrating gaze again and said, "I don't have wants, Doctor Reynolds. I have needs. We all have needs. I need you to put faith in the results you will soon have from the labs of the analysis of those old bones. I need you to have unwavering faith in those results. I need you to be honest with me now, because I know there must be all kinds of theories rummaging around in your scientific head and they must be quite unsettling to you. Perhaps, I can alleviate your concerns. Or, at the very least, point you in a direction that will lead you to a greater understanding."

"And how would you know about any concerns I may have, or how to placate them? What do you know about my discovery?"

"Well, let's see what I know, Doctor. I know, that after five years of trying to secure grants and donations, so that you could return to that lovely valley in France to begin an exploration of another cave, near where you began your career, an anonymous donor suddenly came through with the required funds. No doubt, you believed the money was donated to curry favor with you after your brother had been elected. It would not be unreasonable for someone to believe you could be a valuable conduit to your brother as a way to repay their generosity."

"Was it you who financed the dig?" I asked him. "As a way to curry favor, as you say?" Obviously, I had considered when the money had anonymously arrived last year, that it

68

was to make me feel obligated in some way, or, more likely, it was orchestrated by my brother and he had already done a quid pro quo for my benefit.

"If I wanted an audience, or a favor from your brother, I would have just demanded one," Christ said, not answering my question. "Large campaign donations come with certain benefits. Let's see what else I know, Doctor. I know that I am quite impressed that you found the coffin in the wall."

"It was quite by accident."

"Of course it was. It would have had to have been. Still, quite impressive. I know, that the bones you found in that coffin would have been in wonderful condition in that airtight space. And I know that the bones would not have been intact."

He paused and, leaning forward again on his cane, he said, "And now, Doctor, tell me what else I can tell you about what I know?"

I was mildly upset that one, if not several, of the students who were with me that day, and had been sworn to secrecy, had mentioned the find to others. How else could this old man know such a thing. I had told very few in the

69

scientific community of the find, as I was waiting for verification from the labs, and had only told the dean and several others here at the university. So the old man knew there were bones in the sarcophagus, and that the skeleton was not whole, but still in amazing condition. But did he know everything? Did he know about what was with the bones, because I was the only one who knew that. The students had not been with me when I took it from under the bones.

"Do you know if the bones are Neanderthal? Homo Erectus? Are they early man? How old they are? You seem to think you know so much, Mr Christ, why don't you tell me. Wait, perhaps they are alien. Not of this world. Or better yet, perhaps they are a million years old, left over from an advanced civilization that ruled Earth but became extinct from war or pestilence. I would appreciate any enlightenment you could give me to alleviate all these scenarios that are rummaging, as you say, around in my brain. Anything at all?"

He leaned back in the chair and considered me. "I have heard you can be quite a sarcastic individual, Doctor.

Not an attractive trait in a serious man. But I have also heard that you are a passionate man regarding your profession and that is always a good thing, provided the passion is tempered by wisdom." He then took another business card and a ball point pen from his pocket and scribbled something on the back of the card, placing the card name up on my desk when he was done. Then he looked back up at me. "The rummaging, dear Doctor, is caused by the confusion of the find, not the find itself. Because of all that has been discerned, through all these digs of the past, what you have found does not seem possible, does it? I believe you knew that as soon as you peered inside that tomb. I believe you would have reached into your pants pocket, after the initial shock of the find wore off, and you would have pulled out your little coiled tape measure, and you would have measured the femur bone that would have been laying along side the rib cage. A quick calculation in your head would have caused you to measure the femur again. And it would be then, at that precise moment, that scenarios would have begun their rummaging."

I looked at the old man who sat smugly smiling in

front of me, his right hand resting easily on the ornately carved piece of mahogany that was his cane, and wondered how he could possibly know these things.

"My dear professor, what did your calculations tell you, calculations that I am sure have been verified to be quite accurate? How tall would this man have been - and it was a man - when all the pieces were intact and a full skeleton was housed inside a live body? How tall would that body have been twelve thousand years ago, standing at the entrance to that cave and peering out over that lush valley, my dear Doctor Reynolds?"

Leaning back again in the chair, I contemplated the man in front of me, and I had a powerful feeling that he knew more about the find than even I did. And I had no idea how that could be possible. I decided to answer his query. In a few weeks it would be common knowledge to the world anyway.

"Eight feet, four inches, give or take an inch."

His eyes held mine for several seconds, then he nodded toward the card that lay menacingly on the desk. I looked at that card for several more seconds, then reached over, lifted it and read what he had written.

Again, the painful smile and a slight shrug of narrow shoulders. "Off by an inch," he said. "You, not me."

Leaning back again, I pinched the bridge of my nose with thumb and index finger. The discovery of the sarcophagus was major. The contents were somewhat problematic. Giants buried in impossible secret tombs in a prehistoric time. The whole thing was preposterous, yet here we were. The scientific community would be skeptical, and who could blame them? Hoaxes had been perpetrated before about giants having roamed the Earth in prehistoric days. Amazing finds discovered, with photographs in twenty-five cent periodicals, of massive bones in graves dating back to a distant past when our ancestors had crawled from the fetid swamp and stood on two legs. All debunked, of course, but the stain of their memory still lingered, like the misdeeds done by the black sheep mar the family tree, the passing years unable to fade the stain. My documentation of the dig was complete and precise, but still there would be nay-Sayers, because, as I have mentioned before, we are a jealous lot.

"Why do you say 12,000 years?" I asked.

"Because that is what they are. The labs will verify that."

"I ask again, Mr. Christ, what is it you want?"

"As I mentioned before, Doctor, it is imperative that you believe what the carbon dating will confirm, that the bones date back twelve thousand years. But what is even more important, is that the entire scientific community must also believe it. There will be doubters, that goes without saying, like the climate doubters who refuse to acknowledge scientific evidence of climate change. There is nothing to be done about them. However, I am afraid there will be a large degree of skepticism from respected members of your society of diggers, if only because of the nature of the find. You must satisfy that skepticism, dear Doctor. It is vitally important that the archaeological world is united in agreement regarding your find."

"Why is that?" I asked. "Why should this discovery be any more important than the cave in Neander, or the Denisova cave in Russia. Louis Cartet and his discovery of Cro Magnon. Lucy. All major discoveries that gave us links to the past. Now, maybe we have evidence of a tribe of giants who may have walked among us. Important, yes, if proven true. But why is it so vitally important, as you claim it must be?"

"Good question, Doctor, and one we can discuss further when you return."

I leaned forward, resting elbows on the papers on my desk, glancing at the clock upon the wall.

"There is a half hour before my next class, sir. There is no need of you waiting here until I return from it. Please, answer my question."

Again, that disturbing smile. "No, no, Doctor, once again you misunderstand. I don't mean your return from class. When you return from Brazil. All your questions will be answered when you return from Brazil."

"But I am not going to Brazil. Who told you I was going to Brazil?"

"But of course you are, my dear Doctor Reynolds. You will leave in the next few months and are expected back no later than the end of June. That is very important, Doctor. No later than the end of June."

LEOPOLD CHRIST

I didn't like the path our conversation had now taken. Obviously, I was talking with a slightly deranged elderly man, and despite the pedigree of his sponsor, and the probability that he had financed my dig, my patience with the odd Leopold Christ had run its course.

"I assure you that I have no plans, or intentions, of traveling to Brazil anytime soon. Now, if you would please excuse me, I need to prepare for my class."

The elderly gentleman sat there, impassively looking at me, the skin on his face, it seemed to me, pulling even tighter against bone. Slowly, he reached into his suit coat pocket and retrieved another card and the elegant pen, once again scribbling onto the card. When he was done, he leaned forward and laid the card on my desk, this time with the writing face up.

"What is that you have written?"

"That, dear Doctor, is the verification you will need to prove your discovery in France was no anomaly, no ruse, no fluke."

I looked at the card, then back up at him. "You have written down a set of co-ordinates," I said. "Do they represent somewhere in Brazil?"

"They most certainly do. In the Amazon section of the country. Fortunately, in a part of the rain forest that has recently been destroyed, giving you easy access."

I couldn't help but chuckle at the absurdity. "Easy access to what?"

"I suppose, I could have sent you to Indonesia, but the rain forest there is quite thick. Turkey was a possibility, but they have suddenly become very protective of their antiquities. Somalia seems to be in a little too much turmoil currently. As is Mexico. So Brazil it is."

I smiled at the old gentleman. Obviously, he was off just a little.

"Mr. Christ," I said as I stood, "thank you for stopping by. I really do need to get ready for class."

He stayed seated.

"At those co-ordinates you will find a cave that has been buried in the growth of the forest, perhaps only occupied by local animal life for many thousands of years. There is an indigenous tribe that has ruled that area since migration brought them there thousands of years ago, living their lives little different than their ancient ancestors. Truly remarkable, Doctor, yet not so rare as one may think. In the forests of Indonesia, in certain valleys among the mountains of Tibet, in areas of the African continent, small communities still exist, where the populace live in huts, draw water from nearby streams, start fires with flint, hunt with stone tipped weapons probably dipped in some kind of poison. They know nothing of a modern world."

He then smiled at me and raised a dismissive hand. "I'm not telling you anything you don't already know. These people do not choose to live their lives this way, do they Doctor? They do so, because it is all they know. They have no knowledge of automobiles, guns, malls, electronics. They do not know that their village is but a speck of land occupying a tiny patch on a small orb that spins through the depths of space in a medium sized galaxy. They have no idea that wars have savaged that orb since first they had settled, that disease has ravaged the populace who occupy it, that there are seven billion others living on it who look much like they do, some of whom live in towering buildings. They are completely ignorant of all that is beyond their sphere. They have no knowledge of other languages, flights to the moon, pyramids in Egypt, or Egypt itself."

"Your point?"

"There are very few of these peoples left untouched, in any way, by the outside world. As you know, there were many more a hundred, two hundred years ago, living in the jungles of the Philippines, the mountainous terrain of China, the bush of the upper Nile, the plateaus of Chile. But through expansion of industry, and the ease of motorized transportation, civilization has invaded almost the entire Earth. Eventually, it will all be polluted.

"Now, what has science found, my dear Doctor Reynolds, each time they have come upon an ancient civilization, whether they be extinct or still active? What is the common denominator among them all?"

Slowly shaking my head, I leaned forward once again on my desk. "Are you suggesting that the bones I pulled from a wall in a cave in France are the bones of a god? That this eight and a half foot tall man was a towering god with mythical powers?"

"Those bones are not the bones of a god. You and I

both know that, Doctor. However, the people who lived in that valley twelve thousand years ago, would not. Neither would the hidden peoples of Africa, Tibet or the Amazon. You must go to Brazil, Doctor. It is vital that you do so."

"Why is it vital, sir?" I said, my voice rising a little in frustration with his insistence and his refusal to leave.

He remained calm, and even leaned comfortably back in the chair.

"You will find something in that cave in Brazil that will verify your find in France. It will be the most important discovery ever, even more important than the discovery that things such as dinosaurs once roamed this planet. Beyond that, I can not say anything. I do not want to taint your findings or your methods in any way by telling you too much. It is imperative that this be your discovery."

He then leaned on his cane and came to a standing position.

"I will finance the entire trip, and promise to finance three more excavations of your choosing. You will not need to concern yourself with college students to assist you on the dig. I have hired ten experienced archaeologists to do the work of excavating the cave anyway you desire. Any machinery you want or need will be available to you. There will be a film crew to video the entire process."

"Mr. Christ....."

"Did I mention, Doctor Deiter Von Bratan will assist you?"

"Deiter Von Bratan? From Munich?"

"Of course," Leopold Christ said. "He is very excited to be working with you again and is anxiously waiting to hear from you the details."

"Doctor Von Bratan is one of the foremost archaeologists in the world. He's a legend. Anyone in my field would give their eye teeth to work with him. You have him, you don't need me."

Leopold Christ stood erect and reached a hand across the desk. "I don't exaggerate when I say how vital you are, Doctor Reynolds. And I don't exaggerate the importance of the dig. It must be finished by the end of June."

My mind was racing. The opportunity to work with Deiter again was compelling. The promise to finance three more digs in the future was tantalizing and certainly welcomed. The worst part of the job was begging for money to finance it all, and three digs could consume the next ten years. And the guarantee that the old man was making about verification of the discovery in France was also a powerful incentive.

"I'll have to speak with the dean about a leave of absence," I said. "I'll miss the whole semester."

"Already done," Christ said. "The universities students will be enjoying a new wing to the library in a few years. Do we have a deal, Doctor?"

I frowned, shrugged and reached a hand across the desk to gently shake the elderly man's hand. He possessed a firm, dry grip.

"Yes, we do, Mr. Christ."

"Excellent, Daniel," he said. "Why don't you call me Leo."

five

The doorman wished me a good morning as he opened the door and I entered the impressive lobby of the Hay-Adams. It was just past ten and already the plush seats of the lobby held a dozen well dressed individuals scattered among them, quietly speaking to one another, favors being asked, granted, denied. Under elegant arches and multi-candled chandeliers that led to the elevators, the not so faint odor of power and wealth hung heavy in the air.

The door to the suite was opened in response to my knock by a short, thin, smiling man of indeterminate age. He gave a slight bow and led me through a door in the suite to a large sitting room where Leopold Christ sat at an ornate,

83

round, marble topped table drinking coffee and reading the Post, the remnants of a light breakfast in front of him. He was dressed in an impeccable dark blue striped suit and looked much the same as he had in my drab office five months before, although the brightness of this room, compared to the dim lighting in my office, did seem to add a little more color to his ancient looking face.

"Ah, here you are, Daniel," he said, rising to greet me, folding the newspaper and laying it on the table. "How was your flight?" he asked, shaking my hand with a firm grip.

I shrugged. "Left on time, landed on time. Beyond that, human beings have learned to ask little else of the airlines. Not to lose our luggage is probably expecting too much, as is a decent cup of coffee."

"Well, pour yourself a cup from this pot, my young friend. You will not be disappointed. Best coffee in D.C. Would you like something from room service? I would rather not go to the dining room. We can talk up here."

"No, I'm fine, just coffee," I said, pouring a cup of the dark brew and moving towards a comfortable chair he had indicated near the open window where a warm breeze of a late June morning pleasantly entered the spacious room. The suite had a magnificent view of Lafayette Park, the thick grassed area with thoughtfully situated trees and walkways lined with low beds of flowers that led toward the White House just beyond. In the distance, towering over the office of my older brother, stood the majestic Washington Monument, gleaming in the sunshine from the many years of restoration. And far beyond that tall obelisk, the columns of the Jefferson Memorial could be seen, the statue of the founding father standing ever vigilante in its center.

"Nice view," I said, carefully settling into the chair so as to not spill the coffee. "You know, Leo, considering all the money you have supplied for my digs, I really know nothing about you. I don't even know where you live. For all I know, this could be your residence. In fact, I don't even know what country you are a citizen of. Not that it matters."

Leopold Christ sat opposite me, one knee casually crossed over the other, and regarded me with those intense eyes that now seemed playful. He smiled.

"When first we met, my dear Doctor Reynolds, it was I who was quite content to share some casual banter before getting down to business. Yet, I recall, it was you who wanted to get straight to it. Now, when there are so many important things to discuss, you want to talk about scenery and, perhaps, the weather, too."

I shrugged. "Well, it isn't like we haven't talked almost everyday in the last five months. I've kept you informed every step of the way. So there really isn't anything more I can tell you that you don't already know, other than the results of the carbon testing, which, by the way, I got yesterday."

"And?"

"And what? You know what the report says. You knew what it would say before I flew into Brazil to start the dig." I placed the coffee cup on a side table and leaned forward. "I didn't fly here to give you the results of something you already know. I am here to find out how you knew. I have done what you asked, and now I want answers."

Leopold Christ sat easily in the chair, slowly stirring a small silver spoon in his coffee cup, considering me for a minute or two. Taking several sips, he then asked, "Daniel, have you read Conan Doyle?"

"Sherlock Holmes?"

"Yes."

"Sure. Back in high school. A story or two. Why?"

"Well, Holmes would always tell Watson, 'Watson, when you have eliminated the impossible, whatever remains, however improbable, must be the truth.' Or something to that effect. What truths have you come to the conclusion of, my dear friend, remembering the wisdom of Sherlock Holmes?"

"About the finds or about you?" I asked.

"There is no difference, Daniel. There cannot be. The bones and I are connected. Surely, you understand that now."

Brazil had been no different than France, except finding the bones in France had been accidental, while the bones were what I sought in Brazil. And I found them in the exact co-ordinates Leopold Christ had said they would be.

The excavation was the easiest of my career and Dieter had said the same. That part of the rain forest had, only the year before, been cut down by the companies that were destroying a vital part of our eco-system, and a cave that had been hidden from view for countless years became visible once again. The tribe of people who had inhabited the area for who knows how many years, had moved further into the density, away from the mechanical invasion they neither understood nor could defeat, although some of them had died trying.

With ten young, experienced men to help with the dig, Dieter and I got right to it. I told Dieter very little, wanting him to have no preconceived views on the dig. He, obviously, knew of my find in France - the whole archaeological community was aware of it - and, while he never came out and said it, I felt he was skeptical of the find. Early on he was a little stand-offish, and although we weren't best buds or anything like that, we had worked together twenty years before, had communicated over the years and I considered him a mentor. I thought I had earned his respect during my career, so his attitude was a bit surprising

We conducted the dig as we would any excavation, slowly and carefully working our way through the spacious area of the deep cave, selecting areas in which to excavate, digging into the ground, sifting through the dirt, cataloging and documenting all finds, of which there were many. Most of what we unearthed were animal bones from the upper part of the excavation, along with some stone tips from lower elevations that were very similar to the etched points that had been discovered in digs in the American West, particularly in Colorado. A meter below the current level, near the entrance to the cave, we unearthed a carved piece of ivory. Von Bratan had become very excited about that discovery. That was not something that should have been there, at that level, and the find seemed to rejuvenate his interest in the dig, which was good. He had expected we were there for a similar discovery like I had made in France, and I had sensed this rather mundane dig had been quickly losing his interest.

As for me, I had spent most of my time inspecting every square inch of the rock walls, looking for a line etched into the stone that would reveal another sarcophagus. I didn't find it until the end of May, but find it I did and that now brought a question to mind.

"When first we met in my office five months ago," I said, "I remember you saying that Brazil would be the easiest dig. Easier than Indonesia, safer than Somalia, less disruptive than Turkey. You implied that what was discovered in France would also be present in these other places. Is that correct? Are there other tombs?"

"My young Doctor Reynolds," Leopold Christ said, a smile playing upon those thin lips, "you made a very important discovery in France, and now a second one, exactly like the first, on the other side of a great ocean. The bones you have found in Brazil measured out at almost eight and a half feet, as did the ones in France. The bones, as I have no doubt that report you carry with you confirmed, are 12,000 years old. The method of burial exactly the same, a sarcophagus inserted in a stone wall by means that should have been quite impossible twelve thousand years ago. Brazil has validated France, and it has done so under the co-discovery umbrella of the much respected Dieter Von Bratan."

Stirring his coffee once more, Christ continued. "So, Brazil was a good place to send you. But, to answer your question, yes, the other places would have been just as successful as Brazil in providing validation."

Looking at me over the cup as he sipped, his eyes grew more intense. "My dear, dear Daniel, if we had the time, and, unfortunately, we do not, I could give you the co-ordinates of twenty-five more sites on Earth, beyond France, Brazil, Somalia, Indonesia and Turkey, where you would find the exact same validation."

He frowned then when he saw the stunned look on my face. The excitement of the two finds was disintegrating right before my eyes. It was like listening to the stranger who sits on the stool beside you in a bar, and during the conversation that ensues during the enjoyable evening of drinking and socializing, talking sports, politics, women and adventure, he describes an experience he had one night of watching objects dancing wildly across a desert sky. He has a way with words, and soon you can visualize the UFO's buzzing about the flat lands of New Mexico and you have no problem believing that, maybe, we are not alone. But then he tells you about how they landed and he was approached by short beings, their small mouths in bulbous shaped heads speaking English, and how they all had a very nice tete-a-tete right there in the cool of the evening. And all you can do at that point, is pay your tab, say good night, and leave the bar just as quickly as you can. It was that kind of feeling that washed over me.

"You don't believe me, Doctor Reynolds?"

"Thirty graves?"

"Yes. Some buried in walls of stone, others under layers of dirt, exactly as the two you have excavated. The coffins the exact same dimensions as the two you now have. The bones laid precisely the same as what you have already seen. Precisely the same."

I stared at Leopold Christ for a long time, the skull like face impassive as if he had just said to me, 'I think it may rain this evening'. I believe the human mind can quickly adjust to things that happen when presented to it in small doses. An explosion rips through an apartment building reducing it to rubble, yet we go dashing up the street to see if we can assist in any way. But a tornado levels a town and we stand among the rubble unable to comprehend the destruction. That was how I now felt, trying to make sense of it all. Thirty graves, situated around the world, 12,000 years old.

The tomb in Brazil had almost escaped me. The top etched line was barely above the level of the floor of the cave. Another few inches of sediment and it would have been covered. But I found it, and we excavated that spot. The dimensions were exactly the same as the one in France and we did the same things to it as I had done in France, using the hooks and cement. Only this time I had brought come-a-longs, so sliding the sarcophagus out of the wall was easy. Doctor Von Bratan was ecstatic at the find. At sixty-eight years of age, and almost fifty years of digs in his respected career, he proclaimed it the greatest thing that had ever happened in his life. I allowed my old mentor to pull back the hide that covered the bones, and he did so very slowly, savoring the moment. His gasp was audible when he gazed upon those bones. Everyone on the dig was excited by the find and, later that first evening, while they sat about the fire in front of our tents, drinking and celebrating, I went to the coffin. Secreted in the same space as the one in France, I found an object that was an exact duplicate of the first. Again I was the only person who knew of it, the shiny metal object about the same size and shape as a hand held two pound dumbbell. Even now, almost a year after the first discovery in France, I had no idea what it was or the purpose for it being there. I had had the first one analyzed not long

93

after coming back from France, and the report on it stated that there were traces of eight different kinds of metals in its composition, including the rare metals Rhodium, Rhenium and Iridium. There were three metals that had no name or prior known existence on this planet.

Thirty graves. Composing myself, I asked, "The exact displaying of the bones signifies something?"

"Most definitely, Daniel," Christ said, standing and placing his cup on the table. "The size of the sarcophagus, the exact placing of the femur bones over the rib cage, the angle of the skull and its place of honor just to the left of the rib cage, all signify something. Something quite grand."

"And what would that be?" I asked as he walked by me to stand at the open window.

Gazing out toward the White House, standing quite erect without aid of his cane, Leopold Christ replied, "It signifies that these are the bones of a great warrior." And then he whispered into the breeze, "The greatest warriors the universe has ever seen."

six

Warrior, Leo had said. Not king. Not prince. Not mystical leader. But warrior. I didn't understand. Were they the Knights Templar of the Stone Age? Perhaps they were powerful giant beings, whose prowess in battle led to the legends that future generations would use to create the Titans, eventually attaining god like status in the re-telling. Had they fought together as a unit? How incredibly impressive and daunting they would have appeared to homo sapiens of the day, towering on average three feet over all others, perhaps wielding devastatingly effective weapons But how could that be? The remains of these warriors were scattered among the Earth, not sharing a common land. If they fought separately, as powerful leaders, then who was it they led? Warrior? Warrior for who? Warrior against whom? And how did Leopold Christ know this?

I stared at the back of the old man as he stood by the window and remembered that feeling of dread that had washed over me in my office, back at university, when first I had met Leopold Christ. The same feeling was descending on me once again.

"Do you mind telling me how you know about ancient burial rites? And explain to me 'greatest warriors the universe has ever seen'. I think I would feel more comfortable had you said 'the greatest warriors the world had ever seen up to that point in our history'. I think I am feeling a little uncomfortable, because you said exactly what you meant to say, and now I would like some explanation for all of this. Are you going to tell me what this is about?"

Leopold Christ stood at the window for many long seconds, looking down at Lafayette Park. "This is a fine looking city," he said after a while, "but it lacks the charm of many European capitals." Then he walked back to the round table, pouring himself another cup of coffee.

"I am a very old man, Daniel," he said, as he sat down once again, crossing his legs, "and I have waited a very long time for someone to ask me that question. A very long time."

He sat sipping the coffee, his eyes fixed on a spot somewhere on the breakfast table. When he spoke, his voice sounded different than usual. Older, if that was possible. Distant.

"When I was young, a boy really, I was constantly being academically tested, first by my school teachers, later by people who carried titles that meant nothing to me at the time. I just wanted, yearned really, to have a normal childhood, like the others in my school were enjoying, free from all these time consuming tests, that often my parents and I were required to travel great distances for. By the time of my sixteenth year, I was no longer living with my parents, residing instead in a facility where a dozen of us were undergoing intense training. I guess that is what one would call it if one wanted to be kind."

The coffee grew cool in the cup that balanced on his knee, his eyes closed, face upturned, like he was inhaling a fragrant flower, or remembering a distant past.

"I spent six years in that facility, Daniel, and for the final two years I was the only student still remaining, all the others having been sent back to where they had come from. I was the last one left.

"The days were all alike for me. My teachers, although instructors may be a more apt term, of which there were six, drilled into me each and every day chemistry, biology, psychology, linguistics, mathematics and, perhaps most important, and a very modern term now, analytics. I was made to realize, that if I was to be effective in my assignment, successful in it, even though at the time I knew not what that assignment was to be, and no one was telling me what it would be, I would need to be able to recognize trends. To understand how and why a society was moving in a certain direction. I don't mind telling you now, my dear friend Daniel, that I still remember it to be an exhausting six years. And a lonely six years, too. I had no friends. The other students who were there, until they weren't, could hardly be called friends. We were, as we came to realize quite early on, rivals vying for a singular job, and that competition did not allow for any friendships to develop."

He then looked at me, shrugged and smiled that disturbing grin, and said, "But, I suppose, that also prepared me for my life's work. I have had very few friends and have basically lived a life in isolation for long stretches of time, surfacing when the need arose, ever vigilant to the task others thought me worthy of. For so many years, I have done that task to the best of my ability."   The smile disappeared and his eyes were downcast. "And now, very soon, that task will come to an end, and there is nothing to be done about it. I truly wish it were not so."

He sat still for many moments, his eyes again resting on the round table, a distant look in them.   This talk of tasks had taken him off on a tangent, away from my question about burial rites and warriors.

"You mentioned warriors," I gently said, attempting to bring him back from wherever his mind had taken him. He looked back at me and smiled again.

"Yes. Warriors. I'm sorry, Daniel. Forgive me. My mind was wandering. It seems to be doing more of that with the passing of the years."

LEOPOLD CHRIST

Placing the coffee cup on the table, he leaned forward in his chair and his eyes got back their intensity. "The bones you have so miraculously discovered, my dear friend, are indeed honored bones. They belong to the men who, in this world's greatest hour of need, fought the battles that saved mankind. I believe, and I do not think I exaggerate, that the people of Earth owe their existence to those brave men."

"Leo," I said, as gently as I could after hearing such a statement, "those bones are 12,000 years old. What battles could they have possibly fought that would have saved mankind? And who did they fight them against?"

Leopold Christ leaned back in his chair, the smile returning to his ancient looking face, his hands folded in his lap.

"My young friend, I will now tell you what I know, what has been passed down to me. It is something I could have told you when first we met, but I needed you to witness that the bones you first discovered were not an anomaly, not some poor, wretched creature grown grotesquely large in a world of men under six feet. That there were others and that the care given to their final resting place was, indeed, planned and ritualistic. Do you doubt me, Doctor Daniel Reynolds, when I tell you they were magnificent warriors?"

I smiled patiently at the old man. "Why don't you tell me your story and I will reserve judgment until I hear it. How's that?"

He nodded. "Fair enough, my young friend. But it is a fantastic tale you are about to hear. Your first thoughts will be ones of disbelief. Silly stories, like those told around campfires on cool nights, and being told to you by a senile old man who must surely be delusional. I assure you every word will be true, and more important than you could ever imagine. It is vital that you believe every word."

I sat passively and waited.

"Twelve thousand four hundred and forty-seven years ago," Christ began, "forty-five warriors arrived on Earth to battle for supremacy of the planet."

He paused and waited for my reaction. I made a conscious effort to show none. Deep inside - actually, not that deep - I had expected that this was how he would be explaining it. I think I am more upset with the fact that he is doing so, than I am with the tale I was about to hear. That he

101

would think me so gullible made me angry, but I was prepared for the preposterous, so I had no trouble controlling that anger.

"You don't seem surprised, Daniel."

"I'm not surprised. Not really. Disappointed, yes. But not surprised. Do you really believe extra-terrestrials came to earth 12,000 years ago to wage war on mankind? Were they on a hunt, like in the movie Predator? Did they come for a weekend of sport, and then not be able to leave? Perhaps hundreds of them came for a little paint ball action and when things got out of hand, these thirty died and got buried in the stone of caves to hide the crime. That is if there are thirty. Perhaps, it is just the two."

"Ah, there is the mocking humor of Doctor Reynolds that he is so well known for."

"What do you expect, Leo? Aliens? Battles for world domination? Warriors in tombs? It is all too fantastic. You didn't, couldn't possibly have thought, that I would buy any of this, did you? I am not going to sit here and say life doesn't exist elsewhere in the universe. I have no idea. Have they come to Earth? I have seen no evidence that ever happened. Yet, you want to tell me not only have they come, but they came over 12,000 years ago and they came to save mankind. And you, Leopold Christ, know this to be true. Really?"

"I thought you might be a little skeptical, Daniel....."

"A little?" I said, interrupting him.

He smiled. "That is why I sent you for the second tomb. And, if we had time, we could dig them all up. But we don't. Excuse me one second." Standing, he left the sitting room and went into the bedroom.

I looked out the open window where I could see the top part of the White House. I had plans to meet up with my brother in the evening, to have dinner in the residence and to catch up. I hadn't seen him in over a year, although we had talked several times around the holidays, mostly about our mother, who still lived on her own in a gated community in Florida. He would have a good laugh when I told him of my encounter with Leopold Christ. I could see him now, shaking his head at me, the way he used to do when we were kids and I would do something stupid to piss off our father. It would be worth it to me to suffer the indignity of the head shake, just to hear his laugh again.

Leopold Christ came back and sat down in the chair, laying a leather case about the size of a shaving kit bag in his lap. He raised the index finger of his wrinkled right hand and shook it at me.

"You, my young friend, have not been totally honest with me, have you, Daniel?"

I had no idea what he was talking about and told him so. Then he reached into the bag and lifted out a shiny metal object that was exactly like the two I had in my possession, taken from the two caskets I had unearthed, carbon dated to 12,000 years before this day.

"I have no doubt you have two of these in your possession, Doctor Reynolds. Secreted as they were in the sarcophagus that you pulled out of stone walls. Buried with giants' bones 12,000 years ago. How is it, my dear Doctor, that I have one of these with me now?"

There was only one reason Leopold Christ could have it and that was he had obtained one from a third casket that had been unearthed somewhere else in the world. Maybe there were thirty of these things scattered around the globe.

"Where did you get that?" I demanded. "How long ago did you recover other bones? Was there something in that sarcophagus that you found? Did you find it or did others find it and you purchased the find? Was there some kind of directions or map that told the whereabouts of other graves? What is it you want, Leo? What is it you want of me?" I suddenly felt quite tired.

He frowned. "As far as I know, my young friend, no other graves have been disturbed. Only the two you have now shared with the world. This," he said, grasping in his right hand the thin, smooth cylinder that joined the two conical ends together, "belongs to me. It is mine, and has been ever since I finished my studies and was given my assignment so many years ago."

"What is that thing?"

"Have you had it analyzed, Daniel?"

"Of course."

"And?"

I frowned. "Iridium, Rhenium and Rhodium. Plus three metals not yet discovered on Earth."

Smiling, Christ said, "And probably will never be

105

discovered. This does not come from this planet, Daniel."

"I see," I said, frowning. "And do you know from what planet it does come from? Do you care to share that with me?"

"Of course, Daniel. You need to know everything. This," Christ said, holding up the object, "comes from a world very far from Earth. As does its owner."

^   ^

There was a black bird cawing loudly at the top of the cherry tree outside the open window. The sound of a car horn entered the room. Far off in the distance could be heard the sound of a police siren moving further away from where I sat staring at an old man, trying to contain my temper. He sat staring back at me, waiting for my response to what he had just so simply declared.

I don't think I am angry with Leopold Christ. At least not as angry as I am with myself. I should have seen this coming. I should have been prepared for it. Prepared with a response. But, instead, I just sit here staring at that skull face, deciding if I should even dignify the absurdity with a response, or if I should just rise and leave the suite, putting Leopold Christ in the rear view mirror. Of course, Matthew would tell you, as would our father before him, that I have rarely walked away when I am angry.

"I'm curious," I said, my voice sounding remarkably calm considering how pissed off I was, "is this elaborate and costly ruse an attempt to embarrass my brother, or is it my career you specifically set out to destroy?"

Christ frowned as he placed the device back in the bag and set the bag on the floor at his feet.

"Daniel, if I had come to your office two years ago and said to you, 'Doctor Reynolds, I am from another world and need your help', where would that have gotten me? That you were trying to finance a dig in a place that was one of the sites of the buried bones, was obviously what attracted me to you in the first place. I could scarcely believe that good fortune. I would have financed any expedition to any one of the desired sites, and have, in fact, waited over ten years for someone, anyone, to express an interest in excavating one of those sites. Truth is, I was prepared to do anything I had to do to convince Doctor Von Bratan to put together a dig in the cave in Brazil. I had to do something. Time was running out. Then I learned of your planned dig.

"And can you imagine, Doctor Reynolds, how fortuitous I thought the whole thing was when I learned you were the brother of President Reynolds? Incredible, really."

"And why would it matter who my brother was?" I asked, still in control. "Unless the aim was to somehow embarrass him through me."

"No, Daniel, no. I have no desire to embarrass either you or the President. Or anyone else, for that matter. This is not about you. It is not about him. Certainly not about me."

He looked at me for several seconds. "I understand that you are angry. That you do not believe me. It is fantastic. I grant you that." He smiled. "Remember what Holmes said to Watson, Daniel, and consider this situation and what you know to be fact. There are, in fact, bones buried in crypts that are 12,000 years old. You have found them. This cannot be disputed. They are the bones of very tall people. The crypts have not been inserted into stone recently. The ground in front of them is proof of that fact. You have in your possession, two identical objects that you have taken from these crypts, which means they, too, are at least 12,000 years old. And these objects are comprised of some metals that have never been found on Earth. That, in itself, may not be unalterable proof, but it is compelling."

He paused and leaned forward in the chair, leveling those intense eyes at me.

"At some point, maybe not now, but at some point in the future, the more you consider these amazing finds the easier it will be for you to come to the conclusion that these bones do, in fact, belong to an alien race. There could be no other explanation. And you will, eventually, get your mind around it. It is inevitable.

"But when I, sitting right in front of you, tell you that, yes, the warriors came from another planet, as did I, you dismiss the entire situation as folly. Worse, you claim it to be fraudulent and sinister, despite all evidence to the contrary. Be angry if you want, Doctor Reynolds, but the explorer in you must allow credence to the possibility that I speak the truth."

Leaning back in the chair, I pinched the bridge of my nose and sighed. Everything he said about the sarcophagus

109

finds were true. The bones were 12,000 years old. I couldn't verify to the exact time the crypts were inserted in the wall, but the ground in front of them had certainly accumulated over thousands of years. And those damn metal objects from a time of primitive stone tools. How were they possible?

But there was more to this. Carbon testing had dated the bones. Other tests on the bones provided something else.

"I had other tests done," I said, leaning forward in my seat. "DNA and chromosome testing. The warriors, as you call them, were male, as you said. They were also within one percent of us. Man. Human beings of Earth. How is that possible if they were not born of this world?"

"If you desire, Doctor Reynolds, I can answer all your questions as you ask them. But, with your permission, allow me to tell you why these warriors came to this planet thousands of years ago, and why I, also, came here."

I should leave. I should get up and go. Walk away from a delusional old man who wanted to spin a tale of ridiculous nonsense about ET's and UFO's, like the crazy, bearded, wild-eyed men in blue jeans on sci-fi television. I should leave right now. Instead, I ask Leopold Christ, "What

110

is that metal device you have in the bag?"

There was a slight softening in the intensity of his eyes, and a barely perceptible nod of the head. Reaching down, he lifted the barbell shaped object from the bag, holding it again in his right hand.

"This is a tool, Daniel. It has many uses and many powers, but its power comes from the person who holds it. If I was to hand it to you, you could do nothing with it. If I was to hand it to another who had a similar device, they could do nothing with this one. It responds only to me. To my hand upon it. Specifically, my right hand."

"You say it has many uses. Like what?" The curiosity I had for the metal objects, I realized, was even greater than the awe I felt about the bones.

"With this, I can communicate with anyone who has one of these anywhere in the universe. This device keeps me up to date on my general health. I can even scan others to see if they have an illness. With this, I can modulate a frequency that can cause great distress in others if I find myself in a difficult situation. It is also a powerful weapon. Of course, it would be. It seems no advancement in science

111

or manufacturing doesn't eventually become a tool for destruction. If need be, I could kill with this. But, Daniel, if I were a trained soldier, with this device I could wreak havoc like you could not imagine."

"What, like Darth Vader's light saber?" I said, almost spitting out the words in my contempt for the absurdity of it all.

"This is no silly Hollywood movie, my young friend, with choreographed movements and dazzling effects. I do not sit before you, looking like you because I have morphed from my usual reptile shape into this form. I have not come from the planet Zorn to steal your water supply, Daniel."

"Then why are you here? What do you want? You say you have a story to tell, well, let's hear it. I have a couple of hours to kill. Go ahead, spaceman, weave me a tale."

Leopold Christ leaned back in the chair and regarded me through narrow eyes, a frown upon that wrinkled face. And then he smiled. "Let's begin at the beginning. A very long time ago. A very long time."

seven

"Almost 50,000 years ago something happened that drastically altered the fate of my planet," Leopold Christ said. "First, let me tell you something about the planet where I was born and some of its incredible history."

"Does this planet have a name?"

"Of course. It matters not. Your space telescopes have yet to notice it and the name it is called does not translate into your language. Would you like me to designate a name? Do you have a preference?"

I could not have cared less what it was called. "Continue," is all I said.

"Very well. The planet upon which I was born is quite a distance from here. The galaxy it resides in is younger than the Milky Way by about a billion years. Its' sun is larger than Earth's sun, and not as old. It burns hotter than the one that shines through these windows, but roughly 50,000 years ago scientists began warning of a rising of the core temperature of that heater. They predicted the rising temperature would eventually cause the sun to burn itself out, not in billions of years, but in a relatively short time cosmically speaking. Perhaps it only had millions of years left before imploding.

"Of course, back then, no one became overly concerned about the fate of the planet when they considered it still had millions of years before the end, even though life had already been present for a hundred million years. The people of that time had many other pressing concerns that consumed their thinking. In the recorded history of the planet, this was a time of the greatest conflicts among the peoples of that world, with the threat of annihilation by warring nations a much greater concern than something millions of years in the future.

"Because of its geography, it had always been a world of ravaging conflict even before nations were created. It is a planet slightly smaller than Earth and quite similar. The sky

114

blue, vegetation green. Gases in the atmosphere the same and almost at the same percentages. The land mass covers almost seventy-five percent of the planet and, except for a few islands, the mass is all connected. Much like Earth was before the continents pulled away from each other billions of years ago. There is one great ocean and its water laps the two coasts of the land mass. As you may imagine, Daniel, with no great bodies of water to impede aggression, war was constantly being waged on the entire planet from the very beginning of human life.

"The topography of the planet also provides little resistance to aggression and probably added to it. Mountain ranges dot the land, but they are more like the Appalachian peaks than Himalayan. There is no evidence of there ever being an ice age. Much of the land mass is flat, which made for easy migration. There are no polar ice caps, but the equator is thick with vegetation and it rains almost daily there throughout the year. My world never had dinosaur like creatures of mammoth size and by the time bi-peds came into being, the animals, although abundant and varied, were mostly not carnivorous.

115

LEOPOLD CHRIST

"Can you imagine, Daniel, how it must have been back then? Probably much like what happened here on Earth. A series of transformations among the bi-peds over countless years culminating in man as we now are. The migration that led to the land mass being covered by man, searching for food, searching for more agreeable conditions, searching for something. Always searching. No borders of any kind. But then tribes join together. Societies rise. Culture appears. Farming. Permanence of location. Civility. Laws. Governments. Borders. And with borders, the inevitable disagreements between neighbors that leads to conflicts. Conflicts eventually run their course, as they must, and peace is restored.

"Over countless years of peace the reason for the conflict lies dormant. But then these disagreements flare again, almost like a feud between families, seemingly for no reason what-so-ever. But of course there is a reason. There always is."

Leopold Christ leaned forward , his eyes closed as if he was trying to think of something that had escaped his thoughts.

116

"I believe there would have been two reasons for the endless wars that ravaged that world back then. Imagine you are standing in the land of the east, standing on the border looking into the lands of the west. And in front of you, as far as the eye can see, and a thousand miles beyond, you know that at one time all that land belonged to your country. Some of it may have belonged to ancient ancestors. It was ceded as a condition of peace in some long ago treaty. You would like the land of your ancestors to once again belong to your country. And, of course, after thousands of years of war, this scenario would be played out on both sides of that border. In all probability, no one even knew where that border originally began or ended.

"And then there is the other reason. Pretend that you are Napoleon Bonaparte. Or Adolph Hitler. You are standing on the shore of France gazing across the English Channel. Everything on the continent behind you is yours. Countless miles of conquest to the east. Does that bring you satisfaction? Apparently not. Because, as you stand there, gazing westward across the turbulent sea, the white cliffs of Dover taunt you. They are but a scant few miles from where you stand. You could walk the distance in a few hours. Were it not for the water, your Calvary could charge across the abyss, your tanks could rumble mightily forward, crushing every village on the roads to London. Imagine the frustration that narrow stretch of water created. Imagine how much different the history of Earth would be were there no English Channel. Well, on my planet, when a warlord stood on the border and decided to step beyond it, there was no body of water to prevent his invading army from doing so.

"Easy migration obviously led to conflict, but despite all that warring, or perhaps because of it, technology made progress by leaps and bounds. Bigger and better ways to wreak havoc has always been the catalyst to progress. In a nice reversal of the norm, in that race to destroy one another, something then happened that made all that technology vital to the survival of our species."

Christ stood then and poured orange juice into a tall glass. I declined to have any. I wanted to know about warriors arriving on Earth, and my patience is beginning to wear thin. But, for now, I kept silent.

"Before I tell you, Daniel, about what happened, I must

explain how my planet was situated in its solar system. Excuse me, but rather than keep saying 'my planet', would you mind if I gave it a name? Something simple rather than what the pronunciation of it would sound like in English, which would sound more like a heavy, garbled Russian word."

"Leo, do whatever you want. Just, please, get on with it."

"Good. Then I will choose the name Eden."

I actually laughed. "Are you serious?" I said.

"Quite," he said. "Eden is not the translation of my world's name. Of course it is not. However, there is a place on that world where science has decreed life probably first began, and when peace was finally proclaimed it was decided by those in power back then to name the planet that. Now, while I know Eden is fictitious, it never-the-less fits our needs. And frankly, dear Doctor, I am uncomfortable saying 'my world'. I may have been born there, and spent my first twenty-five years of life breathing its air, but most of my life I have lived on this beautiful planet. I feel more an Earth citizen than an Eden citizen."

"Whatever makes you comfortable," I said. "Please, continue. And get to the point. My patience has limits."

"Of course," he said, leaning back into the chair.

"My planet, Eden, was like all planets. It revolved around its star. Unlike Earth, it lacked a moon revolving around it. However, in Eden's elliptical path were two other planets, both of similar mass to Eden. The nearest was a little over a million miles away from Eden. The other another two million miles beyond. They were both visible to the citizens of Eden at different times of the day or night and, because of the rotation of the planet, they actually went through phases like your moon does with Earth. They really were an incredible sight to see and are probably the one thing I miss most about Eden.

"The closest planet was a desert of rock and dirt. It lacked an atmosphere that was breathable and there was not enough water to sustain life as we know it. It did have valuable minerals, however, that Eden eventually began to mine when they acquired the technology and the need to do so. The other planet was a gaseous body. Uninhabitable. It shone blue in the daytime sky, which made it quite a splendid sight, but it held no other merit than that.

"As I said, the three planets were in the same elliptical pattern around the massive sun, and for billions of years that journey went on without any problems. But then something happened and everything on Eden changed."

Leopold Christ looked at me for many long seconds, a frown upon that Rockefeller face.

"Understand, dear Daniel," he said, "that despite all this warring over all those early years, great progress had been made. There is documentation of life on Eden that goes back almost eighty thousand years. Much of my early education of that history, and the discussion of the teachers and professors that I had, centered on the simple ridiculous documented truths, that thirty thousand years after humans first began speaking sophisticated language, building societies, creating culture and scribbling it all down for posterity, the people of Eden were still at war with each other. History tells us, that fifty thousand years ago there were three great empires on the planet. One in the east, one in the west, and the most powerful one that ruled the northern part of the land. History also tells us, that at that time, all three powers had weapons that could destroy the planet were they to be used, and there appeared to be nothing that could stop the use of them at some point in the future. It was just a matter of time, was the thinking of the day. Much like where Earth is now with nuclear weapons, Daniel. Very similar, actually. And then something happened that, in all probability, saved mankind. Well, at the very least, bought it time.

"Several thousand years after the prediction of a failing sun, which no one on Eden cared about, the desert planet a million miles away, in the same orbit as Eden, was rocked by a massive asteroid that actually threw up a dust cloud that turned the sight of it in the sky red. History tells us that dust cloud lasted over one hundred years. Eden had not yet mastered the technology of space flight, so was not yet mining the planet. That would come many thousands of years in the future. However, scientists of the time spent years monitoring the desert planet, and by the time the dust cloud had dissipated they universally agreed that the asteroid had done more than just send up a dust cloud. It had changed the planet's spin and balance.

"Debate raged for years over what effect, if any, the odd spin might have on the rock planet, even while a massive war was being waged between the powerful army of the North and the army of the East. History records that the leaders of the West just sat back and watched the debilitating war and made ready to conquer both when they were sufficiently weakened by the conflict, having come to the dangerous decision that neither North or East would resort to using their world ending weapons, even in defeat.

"It was then, three thousand years after the asteroid hit, that science united as one and proclaimed to the world that, indeed, the rock planet was spinning erratically. Minutely, to be sure, but there was no doubt. At that point, there was all manner of conjecture as to what that may mean, and the scientific community that had come together as one to tell Eden of the possible danger an erratic spin might pose, fractured again with dozens of theories. Everything from no problem at all to doomsday in the next few years. It was chaos of a very different kind, but chaos just the same.

"Finally, after almost a thousand years of arguing among the scientific community, and at a time when a great plague had decimated the population of the planet, effectively ending North's attempts at defeating East, the data showed, beyond any sensible argument that, yes, the rock planet was becoming unstable. Predictions by the great minds of the time were all the same: the rock planet would continue to spin erratically, the poles would shift minutely over the years, but shift never-the-less, until, eventually, like a spinning top that loses rotation speed, the planet would tilt so much that it would tear itself apart. How much of that destroyed planet would strike Eden was anyone's guess. But all agreed, that enough would smash into Eden to end all life on the planet, even if it didn't smash her apart, too.

"In those three thousand years, while North and East had depleted their assets in combat, West was using their wealth to conquer space. West possessed the greatest minds on Eden, men and women who had escaped the madness of the endless war being waged over the rest of the land. Interestingly enough, minerals that were required for space flight needed to be mined in the East and the money West paid for those minerals financed the war against the North, which kept the war going. When the plague hit, it did not last long, but it was devastating, affecting each region and killing a third of the population of the planet before a cure was discovered. Peace was never declared during this time, but the war was on a sabbatical. It ended up being a thousand year sabbatical."

"When are we getting to the warriors?" I asked impatiently.

"Soon, my young friend, soon. I am explaining why the warriors came to Earth. Listen and you will understand. Shall we order lunch, Daniel? I'm getting a little hungry."

"Order lunch if you want," I said with a shake of the head. "I'm fine. Just get me a coke."

Leopold Christ called the small man into the room and spoke to him in what I recognized as Vietnamese. The man bowed and left the room. Once again, Christ settled back in the chair.

"Four thousand years after the asteroid hit, a man came to power in the West. He was a man of great vision, tenacity and persuasion. With Eden still recovering from the devastation of the plague and the long war, science and technology had shown very little progress during those

125

centuries beyond the space exploration of West. Maybe it was because so many had died, or maybe it was just that everyone was exhausted by the endless wars, but this great man became the one voice calling for reason. Somehow, he convinced the leaders of the three powers to come together to discuss the one simple truth that needed to be addressed, the one truth that must take precedence. It mattered not who controlled the world. When the rock planet came apart all on Eden would die.

"As new generations rose to power over the next thousand years, that one truth led their thinking. Eden evolved. No longer was there a desire by any government to rule over a world that was terminal. How to survive as a species was all that mattered. A council of the three powers was convened to address that problem, and after countless years of negotiations, decisions were made and plans put forward.

"During this time, space exploration had almost come to a standstill. Like everything else on Eden, the plague had impacted its growth, too. But the plans put forward by the council gave priority to space exploration. The precious

126

metal needed to protect the shell of the crafts was quickly exhausted in East. Expeditions were sent to the rock planet in search of more. Eventually it was found in different sections of the planet, and great mining communities were planned and built on the rock planet. You can only imagine, Daniel, the massive undertaking that was. Huge domed settlements where breathable air was made for the workers of the mines.

"Also during this time, over forty thousand years ago, crude space ships were sent to distant galaxies in search of habitable planets. Think of them like the explorers of Earth five hundred years ago, sailing across great oceans into the unknown on tiny ships, many not prepared for the uncertainty of what was out there. Historical records tell us that hundreds of expeditions left Eden in those years, pointed towards worlds that telescopes suggested might prove amenable to our species. Most were never heard from again. After centuries of looking, two planets were found. Earth was one of those two and the only one with life on it beyond vegetation, primitive as it was.

"Does it surprise you, Daniel, that other worlds exist

where life as we know it can thrive? Are you one of those who believe you are alone in the universe?"

I really had never given much thought to alien life. My interest was in the past and the mysteries that it provided. I sought answers to who we are, and who we were, in the rocks and dirt of Mother Earth and saw no reason to look to the skies for answers to those questions. I could get my mind around the idea that life on Earth began in a fetid swamp and through millions of years of evolution took man through ape like body structure into a natural evolution of changes. Homo Erectus, Denisovan Man, Neanderthal, Cro Magnon. Evolution. And all probably begun quite by accident. If someone had told me an accident like that had happened somewhere else in the universe, I probably would have had a hard time believing it. But that is exactly what Leopold Christ was now doing.

"I have never given it much thought," I answered him, shrugging as if to say 'nor do I care'. "I happen to believe that human life began quite by accident. A bolt of lightning electrifying a mass of protoplasm and a single cell gains a spark of life. Who knows how we all came to be? But now,

Leo, you are asking me to believe that the same thing happened on other worlds, which is a stretch for me. And that that protoplasm ended up looking exactly as our protoplasm. You can see where I, or anyone else for that matter, might have some doubts with your story."

"Of course," Christ said, nodding his head. "What are the odds? Astronomical I would think."

Just then the small man wheeled in a tray with Leopold Christs' lunch. He handed me a Coke.

"Ah, I am famished," Christ said, lifting the silver cover off a steaming plate of cooked summer vegetables. "My dear friend," he said, stabbing at a piece of zucchini, "you must always remember the advice Mr. Holmes has given us. When everything else has been eliminated, what remains is the truth. Remember that when you have doubts." While he ate sparingly, Leopold kept up a running dialogue about the importance of eating healthy. Meat, poultry and fish had no place in his diet. Neither did salt or spices. He said he particularly enjoyed white rice. I really could not have cared less about any of it.

^   ^

LEOPOLD CHRIST

"That was wonderful," he stated, as he pushed back from the tray table, less than half the meal eaten. "Now where was I in the narrative?"

"You were in the middle of telling me the history of your planet," I said, "and frankly it may be an interesting story, but I am no longer interested. Fine, your space probes found Earth. Got it. Why were eight and a half foot men sent here 12,000 years ago? That is all I'm interested in. That's it."

He frowned at me. "You are a man in the middle of your life, my young friend. You have the benefit of many years of life still ahead of you. I am a very old man. Very few years left for me. One would think, if impatience was to be attributed to one of us, then it would be me who would exhibit it."

"The bones, Mr. Christ. Explain to me about the bones."

"What about me, Doctor Reynolds? Is there no curiosity as to why I am here on Earth?"

"There certainly would be," I said, "if I was convinced that your story is true. I am not. Tell me about the bones.

130

Maybe that will convince me. And then I'll be curious about where you came from and why. The bones, Leo."

He stared at me for several seconds, then smiled and gave a slight bow of the head. "As you wish," he finally said.

"The warriors came into being on Eden almost twenty thousand years ago. After thousands of years of peace and prosperity on the planet, the ruling councils of the time found it necessary to place unpopular restrictions on the populace. These restrictions caused quite a bit of unrest, and rebellion against authority became a serious problem. The warriors were the solution to the problem."

"What kinds of restrictions?" I asked.

"Oh, there were several. During the thousands of years of war and strife, the constant destruction and chaos, the average life span for man was forty-two and a half years. After two thousand years of peace, along with great strides being made in medical science, the average man could expect to live just beyond one hundred years. As you might imagine, Daniel, a hundred generations later and the population on the planet had grown to unsustainable levels for the natural resources that Eden could provide. At that point, the council

131

decreed that all women would be limited to one birth during their lifetimes. Immediately after the delivery of a healthy baby the uterus was removed. As you may imagine, this was not popular with the people. From all reports that I have read from that time, it was a desperate attempt and it was desperately needed. Time passed, and while it was never a popular law, people did eventually accept it as the norm. That was until reports began to circulate that the privileged of Eden had no such restrictions placed upon them. That, and the growing disparity of wealth that grew greater every century, led to civil unrest.

"You must understand, Daniel, that unlike Earth, Eden had no real poverty anywhere. The councils had made sure that all citizens could live a sustainable level of a comfortable life. But, as we know, the perception is that the grass is always greener somewhere else. Small rebellions began in remote rural communities that were quickly put down by local law enforcement. But the seeds were sown, and as the years passed, new generations continued to lift the banner of social unrest. Eventually, it became too much for the local authorities to contain. It was then the idea for the warriors came about. Through a mutation of genes, babies were born who grew to a greater height than the average person. And then, when those babies grew into adulthood, they were impregnated with mutated sperm that would bring forth life that would also grow to a greater height. Five generations later, the eight and a half foot average height was attained.

"This was all done in total secrecy of course, in a very controlled setting in a rural part of the western province, where centuries before other secret endeavors had been conducted. The men and women of five generations were not allowed any interaction with the outside world. Hundreds of families were part of the experiment. When the fifth generation of children reached thirteen years of age, they were taken from their families to begin intense training that would eventually make them fierce warriors. Armed with powerful weapons, they were sent to regions where civil unrest was a problem. By all accounts, the warriors were effective in quelling every rebellion on the planet. Their brutality became legend. And they answered to no one but the council."

"But why did they come here? Why the hell were they

on Earth?"

With a heavy sigh, Leopold Christ leaned forward in the chair and frowned at me. "They came to Earth to do what they did best, Doctor Reynolds" he said. "They came to kill."

eight

She stood knee deep in the cold water of the stream, the current strong but far from raging. Her skin tingled from the brusque rubbing she had given it during cleaning. She so enjoyed the feel of the sun on her drying skin, while at the same time her long damp hair clung to her shoulders and back. Three different sensations on her naked body - the cold of the water on her legs, the damp of her hair on shoulders and back, the drying warmth of the sun on breasts and stomach - that blended into one pleasant sensation. Beside her, the child was just squeezing the water from her hair and shivering slightly in the cold water. Smiling down at the little one, she nodded toward the bank of the stream and they moved onto dry land. Slipping into a long white robe, she noticed three deer by the edge of the woods gazing at them curiously. She turned her daughters attention towards them and the child smiled.

She picked up a large bowl she had carved from wood and the two of them began walking across the tall grass towards the edge of the woods where blueberry and raspberry bushes were heavy with ripeness. They would make a satisfying morning meal for her mate and son who were probably still asleep. The child ran ahead of her, moving toward the deer who warily watched her advance and then bounded off when she got too close. The child called out for them to come back and the mother smiled.

Together they filled the bowl with fruit, the air heavy with the smell of their ripeness, taking their time, enjoying the warmth of the rising sun. Later in the day, while her mate would be away from their home, she was planning on showing her daughter the way to carve out a bowl like the one they were now filling. She had found a perfect piece of wood for it just the day before.

With the bowl full of berries, she took her daughter's

hand and began walking toward their home at the base of the mountain. It was little more than a hut, and very small for the four of them, but she was quite happy to be out of the damp cave. She would enjoy it while she could, knowing that they soon would be leaving this valley.

Coming around a clump of trees, they began up a gentle rise when suddenly a large group of men stepped out from the trees and blocked their path. The woman, much taller than the brutish men, looked down on them while she maneuvered the child to a position behind her. The men carried spears in their powerful hands. Their short, stocky bodies formed a wall between her and where she was going. There was much grunting from the men, their large sloped heads bobbing in rhythm, feet stomping the ground. She looked for a place to flee, but saw none.

The large group was agitated. They all looked toward their leader who stood staring at the tall, thin woman with the light colored hair, thin nose and soft rounded chin. The child who stood beside her had a similar face. Slowly, he began walking towards her. His arms and chest were bare, hairy and heavily muscled. He had painted black stripes on his

137

forehead and body. His nose was very large and flattened against a heavily bearded face, his brows quite prominent, the eyebrows thick.

With an extended hand, she backed the child away from her and then stood motionless, waiting for the man to approach. She had no weapon other than herself, but that would be enough to kill him. She could not defeat two dozen armed men, but she would kill the man who approached before the others could come to his rescue.

The man was a short distance from the woman and child, moving confidently towards them, when a loud sound reverberated through the valley, echoing off the mountain and tumbling through the forest. It lasted but a few heart beats. The men turned toward the mountain and saw a lone man walking towards them along the top of the grassy rise. Their grunting became louder, their agitation grew greater. He moved slowly, standing upright in a non-aggressive manner. He was tall, much taller than them, and he wore a long, flowing blue cloth that was unlike anything the men had ever seen. His face was hairless and the hair on the top of his head was long and the color of bone. They could see he was carrying something in his hand, but it looked non-threatening and caused them no concern. As he got closer, they could see that he had facial features like those of the woman. His arms were long and lacked the muscle that those in front of him had.

The leader turned his attention from the woman to the man who drew nearer. Moving quickly to stand in front of the others, he held his spear out in a threatening gesture. Behind him, the grunting got louder and more intense. And still the man approached.

From just beyond the range of a tossed spear, the man came to a stop and looked down at the brutish men below him. He looked for the prominent brow, the slope of the forehead, the massive mandible. Features these men possessed. Slowly, the tall man raised his hand toward the group. In his hand he held something that was small and shiny, the sun reflecting off of it like it reflected off certain rocks in the mountain. When he did this, the woman took the child's hand and led her into the clump of oak trees.

The leader grunted loudly and began to charge at the man, all of the men behind him following him up the hill in a rampage, loud grunting accompanying each stride of their short legs. When they were half way to where the man stood, a harsh, intensely bright beam of bluish tinted light erupted from the object, and with a flick of his wrist the beam arced across the advancing charge. The thin beam lasted less than a few heart beats, but every body part of the charging horde swept by the beam fell to the ground and, in an instant, the grassy rise was covered with severed arms, legs, heads and torsos, the ground quickly becoming a dark red patch from blood that gushed from massive wounds. The men who were not yet dead lay howling on the ground dying. Only one brute still stood on that rise, untouched by the beam. He stood in horror at the carnage, looked up at the tall man who pointed his weapon at him, then dropped his spear and ran down the hill, past the woman and child, and into the woods.

The woman and child came out of the trees. She carried the bowl of berries easily in her left hand and held the child's hand in her right as the two of them walked a path that led them away from the dying and dead. By the time she reached her mate, the last of the moaning had stopped and the hillside was quiet. Above them, large birds had already begun to circle the killing field.

Without a word, he turned and walked back in the direction from where he had appeared, the woman and child walking behind him.

∧ ∧

After sharing the berries with his mate, daughter and son outside their shelter, the tall man walked back to where the severed bodies lay on the grass, rotting in the heat of the day. Hundreds of birds were hopping among the dead, ripping at the flesh and then quickly dancing away from the carnivorous beasts that had been drawn to the carnage. There was much growling and hissing as he walked past, but none of the feasting animals made a move towards him.

Crossing the field, he walked to where the lone survivor of the slaughter had entered the woods. Tracking the fleeing man was easy. He followed the track to a dense growth where crude, inefficient shelters stretched over a short distance, and he heard a commotion that brought him to a large clearing of flattened down grass where the men of the tribe stood in apparent agitation. Two of the men stood in the center of the commotion, animated and vocal, stomping

141

on the ground with short, powerful, thick legs, flailing their muscular arms above their large heads. The women of the tribe stood in a semi-circle on the outside of the men and they were very loud with their moaning, wailing and grunting. Beyond them, on the far edges of the clearing, stood the children, silently watching the group of men. Standing at the edge of the trees, he watched the feverish activity, listened to the nervous speech he did not understand and felt no particular emotion that he was the reason for it. Eventually, he was noticed.

The men all turned to see what one of them was pointing at and a deathly silence fell over the area. The leader of the tribe had died on the hill that morning and no one had come forward yet to claim leadership. The men looked to one another, agitated and unsure what to do. The women crowded together and stared up at the tall man covered in a blue cloth they had never seen before. He appeared to have no weapon and they wondered why their men did not attack and kill him. The oldest woman of the tribe sat on a log beyond the curious children and looked up with her one good eye at the strange man. She had protested to the leader the tribe's settlement in this valley after the difficult trek over the mountains. She had warned the leader there was danger in this valley. There was evil. There had been horrible death here. She had sensed it. The trees of the forest had told her these things. They should not stay here, she had told him. But he would not listen to the warnings of an old woman. He saw no danger. He saw there were many animals to hunt. He saw there was a forest for shelter. He saw a place to rest after a long migration. He would not listen to the concerns of a crazy old woman. Sitting there, looking at the man at the edge of the trees, she remembered the scorn in their leaders eyes when she had warned him. He was so young, she thought. So brave. So foolish. And now he was dead. Soon they would all be dead. She saw it then and she knew.

One of the men stepped out in front of the group. His height was less than most of the others. He was wide, very muscular, with powerful looking shoulders. He handed his weapon to another and looked up at the strange man. Then he began walking towards him. The tall warrior watched him advance across the clearing, all the while his eyes searching the entire settlement. When the man was several strides away from the tall stranger, he stopped and stared up at him. He saw the shiny object and he knew what that weapon could do to men. Looking into the stranger's eyes, he slowly raised his hands and extended his arms away from his body. And then he bowed his head towards him. And then he stood motionless.

There was complete silence now in the camp. Looking over the man's bowed head, the tall man looked down to the group of men who stood watching him. Some of them laid their weapons on the ground and mimicked the pose of the man who stood in front of him. Some did not. Very slowly, he also raised his arms out to his side, as they had done. There came a few grunts from the men. And then, suddenly, a blast of light exploded through the chest of the short man, catapulting what was left of his body to the edge of the circle of men. There was just a moment of shock from the tribe, then some of the men began to charge at the tall man. Others began to flee toward the trees. The women began screaming and running toward where the children stood in frightened shock. The old woman folded her hands in her lap and awaited death.

The tall man began advancing toward the center of the clearing and the charging, shouting, angry men, his hand moving in long back and forth arcs in front of him, the powerful blue tinged light slicing across the width of the area, severing everything in its path. By the time he reached where the men had been standing, all the men of the tribe were dead or dying. Two had managed to reach the edge of the trees before being severed at the waist.

The women screamed and ran, scooping up their children, attempting to reach what they hoped would be the safety of the trees. The warrior turned towards them and once again unleashed the intense beam. There was no escape for those who ran. There was no mercy for those who fell to their knees in front of him and begged. Some of the children still stood by themselves, crying for their dead parents, in shock and too frightened to move. He stared into their confused eyes. They were the last to be killed.

He stood in the center of the clearing, among all the dead, slowly scanning the area. It was then he saw the old woman, sitting on a log at the edge of the trees. He stared at her until all the crying and moaning of the dying ceased and the area was silent once more. And she stared back at him. She never moved, even when he raised his weapon one more time and aimed it at her. They stood looking at one another for several more moments, and then a blast from his weapon hit her in the chest and sent her crashing into a tree where she crumbled to the ground and never moved.

Satisfied all were dead, he turned to go back to his shelter. From the corner of his eye he saw the man standing at the edge of the trees. Quickly, he raised his hand once more and aimed his weapon at him. But then he saw the man's face. The flat forehead. The thin nose. The jutting chin. It was a face he had seen once before. He stared at the man, who just stood there slowly scanning the entire killing field, the pitiful cries of the dying that had brought him there no longer echoing through the forest. Eventually, his gaze came to the tall man who had caused so much death. The tall man lowered his weapon, turned and walked into the woods.

Drak watched the man who had saved his life many seasons before, walk into the woods. Then he looked back at

146

the dead. Drak stood there until the circle of light began to dip below the top of the trees.

       ^   ^

In the dimming light of the day, the warrior stood by the side of the mountain before a massive rock. Lifting the shiny object toward the stone, a light suddenly shone from it and a topographical map of the area filled the flat surface of the stone. A small blue circle in the lower right side of the map indicated his position. Many small red circles indicated where human life form habitats had been identified six years before during their entrance to this strange world. The map that he gazed upon was the area of this world that was his responsibility.

His mission, for the remainder of his life, was to kill all people who looked like those he had slaughtered that day. It was what he had been doing for six years. Three tribes no longer existed and the tribe who occupied the cave in the valley beyond the mountain could now prosper peacefully because of it. It was now time to journey on.

"Where shall we begin?" the woman asked, as she stood beside him looking at the map.

He pointed to a red circle that was on the far right edge.

"We go here," he said. "North. And then move across the land toward the west."

Walking up to the wall, he pointed to a red circle near the center of the map. "By the time we reach this area," he said, "the boy will be a man."

She nodded. There was much that had to be done to prepare the boy for what he would need to do during his life.

"Do you know what this is, Ethra?" he asked, indicating a dark area on the far left of the map that held no circles.

She shook her head.

"It is ocean," he said, smiling at her. "You have never seen an ocean, have you?"

Again she shook her head, a smile playing upon her soft features.

"Have you?" she asked.

"Once," he said. "From high above when we flew into a disturbance in the lower regions of the East. Water as far as you could see to the horizon. We all just looked out the windows in silence and stared."

He looked at her then. "I will take you to this ocean,

148

Ethra. You will step into its water. Bathe in it. We will live near it for a while. Would you like that?"

She smiled at him. "Yes, I would like that very much."

"Good," he said. "But first, we must move toward the north and continue our mission. We leave in the morning."

She nodded. "I have liked it here," she said. "This valley is quite lovely in the morning when the sun shines through the trees and the mist hangs low over the land. The water of the stream is always cool. There is always a pleasant scent on the breeze. At first I didn't think I would like being here, but now I will miss it."

"When the time comes," he said, "we will return here. I, too, have grown fond of this valley. We will see it again."

nine

"**K**ill who? And why?" I asked. "Surely, a civilization that can send crafts through space and has mining colonies on distant planets, would find little problem defeating the people of any planet they decided to invade. What possible reasons could there be to send assassins here 12,000 years ago to kill primitive man? That makes no sense."

"Quite the contrary, my young friend," Leo said. "Allow me to go back in time, before the warriors, a time you had me omit in your impatience to know about the bones, and all will become clear."

I lifted my eyebrows, shrugged slightly and looked at my watch, indicating he could continue as he wished, but I was growing impatient.

He nodded. "Going back to the time when the two planets were discovered, planets that could support the people of Eden when the time came that we would have to leave, it was decided, that of the two, Earth was the least palatable, but the most promising. The other planet was closer to Eden and had no human life forms, which was considered a plus by some. But it had no animal life forms either, which would mean transportation there of our animal herds. That really was not much of a problem. They could be brought there in small numbers and over the centuries they would proliferate naturally. However, that planet was still being disturbed by volcanic eruptions that our scientists predicted would likely keep occurring for another several hundred thousand years. Well beyond the time we had left before we would need to leave Eden. Even though Earth was in the final stages of the last Ice Age, there was still much land mass free of ice, and volcanic activity was rare. So Earth was chosen.

"Many expeditions were sent to Earth over the years. Neanderthal Man ruled the planet at the time. They were rugged individuals, as you well know, Doctor.   Much larger and brawnier than we were, certainly.   Over many centuries of studying them, their habits, their way of life, it was determined that they had been around for at least several hundred thousand years, but in all that time had made very little progress, which meant they had limited intelligence. Their tools and weapons were basic and had evolved little over countless years. Their brain capacity was quite large - larger than ours - but obviously there was not much activity going on in there.

"During the centuries that we observed them, their numbers grew considerably. They expanded over the land quickly in those years.   An ever growing population searching for food. By the time we first came to Earth, Neanderthal were aggressive hunters and not just scavengers. Their methods for hunting were not particularly well thought out, but they overcame their lack of planning just by shear numbers engaging the prey. They did the same in battle. Inhabiting the planet around that same time, as you know, was another group of homo sapiens that have been designated as Denisovans. We regarded them as being a small threat. Living as they did in the areas of receding ice, their numbers were small. And over a span of a few thousand years, as Neanderthal expanded, they basically wiped out the Denisovan population, forcing the remaining tribes to flee eastward where they eventually died out. The Neanderthal people were fierce fighters, but, even though their numbers were large, it was determined they would not pose a threat to the migration of those who have been called Cro-Magnon man. That assessment eventually was proven wrong. Also of concern at the time, were the animals that heavily populated this world. Massive creatures. Much larger than any we had on Eden. And they were aggressive. Very much so. The feeling at the time was they would provide a constant food source and eventually their numbers would shrink to a level that was not threatening. Another assessment that proved inaccurate."

Leo smiled then. "It is interesting to note, my young friend, that if the destruction of Eden had been imminent, and an exodus of the planet had begun, Neanderthal Man would have been the perfect species for us to have here. You must realize, the people of Eden were leaving a world that even

153

then was far more advanced than Earth is today. Magnificent cities of great beauty and function. Modes of transportation and communication even then that were far more advanced than what is available on Earth today. A life filled with a myriad of amenities that made living quite easy and comfortable. Coming to a planet where the people still lived in caves and hunted with spears and were mystified by fire, certainly could not have been appealing. But the survivors of Eden would carry with them across the galaxies the technology needed to build the world of Eden here on Earth. And, of course, it would have been the slave labor of the brawny Neanderthal that would have done the work. But there was time. Thousands and thousands of years of time. Time for a civilization to prosper. Time for a planet to populate, culture to expand, cities to rise. And it was hoped, by the time we would have to leave Eden, we would be coming to a world at least modern enough that the technology we would bring with us would be easily adapted.

"After thousands of years, reports brought back to the councils indicated that life on Earth was not progressing at a rate that had been hoped for, or expected. The council decided something must be done. Having determined that Neanderthal Man was retarding the progress of advancing civilization, the council found a new use for the warriors. Even though the uprisings had been dealt with quite effectively, the council had still kept the warrior program in existence, although in smaller numbers. Enough to remind everyone that rebellion would be harshly dealt with, but not enough that authority need fear a revolt in the ranks of the warriors. Forty-five warriors, along with their mates, were sent to Earth."

"And they were sent here to kill? Is that what you are saying, Leo? Terminators? Really?"

"The council at that time felt they had no other options," Leo said with a shrug. "All along, for almost thirty thousand years, the thought was that Cro Magnon would proliferate to numbers that would eventually rival those of Neanderthal. When that happened, it was expected their intelligence would then be the deciding factor in a battle for supremacy of the planet. The masters of Eden, knowing the history of their own planet, knew that the struggle for man to conquer Earth would be a long and difficult one, but that eventually it would be won by intelligence, not by brawn. However, after almost thirty thousand years, Neanderthal Man was still the dominant species. Cro Magnon was still living in caves, their tools were still primitive, and while their migration from the depths of Africa had brought them north into what is now Europe, and east across Asia as they followed the receding ice mass, that migration had left their tribes insufficiently populated to seriously combat the Neanderthal. It had been hoped, by every council on Eden, that man would be aggressive as their numbers grew and they would gain dominance over Earth and eradicate the brutish Neanderthal. That hope was not being realized. Cro Magnon, left on their own, would not win the planet. And time was running out. New scientific data on the rock planet's rotation predicted the planet had less than fifteen thousand years before destroying itself. Maybe as few as twelve thousand years if a degree of lean was reached that caused the lean to accelerate. There were many scientists at the time that felt that would happen."

"But man did win the battle," I said. "Neanderthal ceased to exist and man took over the planet. That is documented. We know this, Leo."

"That is very true, my dear friend. Quite true. But they needed help to do it."

"So," I said, "the eight and a half foot men were sent here to help early man defeat the not very intelligent Neanderthal. Forty-five big guys, armed with some kind of magical weapon, to wipe out an entire planet of cavemen. But why stop with Neanderthal? Why not wipe out every human and start fresh with Edenites when the time came for you to leave Eden? Why would such an advanced civilization want to come to a world with such primitive people? Hell, I would think even Earth people of today would seem primitive to such star voyagers as those from Eden. Why not just wipe us all out and have the place to yourselves?"

Leopold Christ stared at me from across the room. His body looked small and withered in the cushions of the chair. The color that had tinged his wrinkled cheeks was now gone, the face ashen once more. Even the intensity of the eyes had dimmed.

"My dear Doctor Reynolds," he said, his voice barely

above a whisper, "for thousands of years that was the exact sentiment some council members exhorted. It is a sentiment still shared by some to this day. It is the reason I, and those who came before me, have been sent here. To try and save mankind, Daniel. It is possible we have failed. I have failed."

∧   ∧

"Those who came before you?" I said, and I couldn't help shaking my head.

Frowning at me, Leo asked, "Why do you not accept what is so obviously clear, Daniel? You have their bones. You have in your possession their weapons. Weapons composed of metals not of this world. Bones unlike any ever discovered before. Me, sitting here with the same kind of weapon and knowledge of things no one should know. Why can't you accept what it so blatantly obvious?"

"Simple," I said. "I have never seen a UFO. I know no one who has. I base my beliefs on facts, Mr. Christ. What I have seen and what has been proven and documented. I don't have the time or the temperament for wild claims and unproven hypotheses. To me, everything is black or white.

158

Conjecture is gray. Wild claims are gray. Bigfoot, Loch Ness, Roswell all gray."

"But you have the bones, Daniel."

"Yes. But that doesn't mean they have to be extra-terrestrial. How can they be? Documented to 12,000 years ago, yes. But also tested to be within one percent of man. Earth man, Leo. This planet. Not some far off doomed planet. That is fact. That is documented. And as far as the metal object that you claim is some kind of an advanced weapon, which I can not imagine it being, true there may be three metals not of this world according to the PMI test, but that just means they have yet to be discovered here on Earth."

"But how did they end up in the coffins, Daniel?" Leo asked, a smile on his face, eyebrows raised.

Reluctantly, I stated, "I don't know. And it is becoming obvious to me that you don't either. First, you claim there are thirty tombs around the world exactly like the two now found. Yet you now mention forty-five warriors were sent to Earth. Where are they buried, Leo? What happened to them? Did they do their job and go home? Back to Eden? Back to a far off planet after killing off an entire population

159

of Neanderthal? Did you seriously think I would believe any of this?"

He stood again and walked past me to stand by the window. Looking out over Lafayette Park, with his back towards me, he said, "With all of the discoveries you archaeologists have unearthed in the last two hundred years, your kind have pieced together what you perceive to have happened in prehistoric times. You really have no way of knowing, though, do you Doctor Reynolds? Some bones are found. Some primitive tools. Carbon dating is done. More bones found elsewhere. More carbon dating. And so forth. And through all these different finds, and all this carbon dating, and all the papers written and theories tossed about, history is written."

Turning to face me he said, "That history, Daniel, you believe, don't you? Yet now, you have discovered something that can completely alter what is perceived to be the truth from 12,000 years ago, and you turn a blind eye to it. I once told you that your discoveries were more important than the discovery that dinosaurs once populated this planet. I told you your discoveries were the most important ever to be

160

found. You have the proof and you question it. Why?"

Leaning back in the chair, I squeezed the bridge of my nose with thumb and index finger. Spaceships and spacemen. I really am having a hard time with all of this. Leo is correct. The giant bones and the metal object buried as they were presents a real mystery. An alien presence would certainly explain things nicely. I just can't accept it.

"Tell me about the warriors," I said, my head leaning back into the cushion of the chair, my eyes closed.

"As I have mentioned," Leo said as he made his way back to his chair, "forty-five were sent here to Earth. They had three missions that they were charged with. First, seek and destroy all Neanderthal life they could. Continue to do that for the rest of their lives. That was the primary objective of them coming here. More than likely they would not kill all Neanderthal, but those not destroyed would pose no serious threat to tribes of Cro Magnon. At least that was the thinking back then. And just so you understand, my dear friend, once someone from Eden set foot on Earth there was no going back to Eden. Remembering the devastation of the plague from the distant past, the scientists of Eden cautioned that there was no way to know what pathogens might be brought back if any were allowed to return.

"The second objective, in hindsight, was quite brilliant. The warriors were sent here with mates. On first reflection, it would be assumed the reason for that was so they would have companionship. Not entirely true. It was so they could reproduce. Grow in numbers. This was very important."

"And why would that be important?" I asked. "Were they to carry on the battle of extinction of an entire race?"

Shaking his head slightly, Leo said, "No, Daniel, not at all. The third objective in the mission was to teach the children, and further generations, the skills that they would need so they could teach man how to begin to live outside the cave. Better methods of hunting with more effective weapons so that fewer hunters died during the hunt. How to farm the land may have been their most valuable instructions that they taught man. Construction of huts. Better tools. A sense of the world around them. A broader vocabulary. A meaning to numbers. I imagine it would have been like teaching babies, except harder because they were dealing with established ways of doing things."

He looked at me then. "Can you imagine, Daniel, how it must have been?"

"Sure," I said. "Without the brilliant help of space travelers the poor brains of early man would never have developed enough to peel a banana let alone leave the cave. We owe everything to your people, Leo. Earthlings should erect a monument to show our gratitude, forgetting for the moment that an entire species was wiped out. Perhaps an ode to genocide could be commissioned by a great poet. Songs sung, books written, by a grateful people."

Frowning at me, Leopold Christ said, "Cro Magnon had been around for thirty thousand years and had hardly made any progress except growing in numbers and migrating north. Maybe they needed a little prodding, Daniel. Regardless, that was the plan. But, as with all plans, not everything went smoothly. You wondered what happened to the other fifteen warriors who came to Earth. Where are their remains? What became of them? We have no idea."

"But you know where thirty are. Why not all of them?" I asked.

"Because we can track their personal device. The

163

device I have tells me where the others are."

"So you knew I had two of them in my possession?"

"Of course."

"Yet you say these things are weapons. Capable of terrible destruction. Did you not have concern I might unleash its power, accidentally?"

"Impossible," Leo said. "As I have said, each weapon was coded to only respond to that warrior. Like the identification systems now available on Earth today that scan eyes or read finger prints. Well, these devices go beyond that. They read finger prints, but also the bio-rhythm of the person holding it. The entire genetic make-up of the person. So there isn't anything you could do with those devices. And neither could anyone else. Which is why they were buried with the warriors. Not only as an act of respect, but because they were useless to anyone else."

"Why can't you track the other fifteen?"

"Probably because they were destroyed. Most likely by their owners."

"And why would the warriors destroy them?" I asked. "This was the weapon they were going to use to wipe out

Neanderthal. Right? How would they do that without their magical weapon, Leo?"

He frowned at me again and shook his head slowly. "You are being quite difficult, Doctor Reynolds. Quite difficult, indeed. Alright. As I have mentioned, not everything went smoothly.

"The first generation of warriors who were sent to quell the rebellions on Eden carried similar weapons. Not quite as sophisticated, or as small, but very powerful. Mostly, the device was simply used as a weapon and could do little else. Over time, the device evolved into being an all purpose tool. Somewhere along the way in its development, it had a chip implanted in it that could be triggered to shut the whole unit down. The weapon had become such a potent tool of power that, fortunately, someone had come to the realization that should the warriors decide to use it for nefarious reasons they could wreak a great deal of havoc. A simple code could render the unit useless."

"Are you saying that is what happened here?" I asked, smiling. "A third of your stellar policemen went rogue? The Stasi no longer under the command of the Fuhrer?"

Again Leo shook his head, but this time he smiled. "Well, we can't be certain about all of them, but, yes, according to the historical reports I have read, some of the warriors developed different plans once they got to Earth. Or soon after. And the code needed to be used. Once the unit was shut down, the warrior would realize the only use it then had was it could be tracked. At that point, they would find that to be a liability."

He stood again and walked to the window. "The parts of this world that were inhabited is where the warriors were detailed to. They each had their own grid to operate in and their own plan of attack. Simple really. Sweep forward. Always forward. It was an attempt to force the Neanderthal into a migration that would bring them to a point at the end of the grid, whether through their attempt to flee an enemy they could not defeat or through starvation. You see, Daniel, as the warriors moved ever forward they were destroying whole herds of animal life, too. You want to know why ancient animals no longer exist, Doctor? They were slaughtered. And not by the Neanderthal or man."

Leo turned towards me, but his eyes did not meet mine.

166

"The woolly mammoth were chased across the expanse of Asia where they crossed into North America, crossing what is now the Bering Sea. They crossed over the receding ice sheets, and they migrated over dry land of a world where the sea level was four hundred feet below what it is today. Behind the mammoths came the Neanderthal. And behind them the warriors. The last of the great herds of mammoths were destroyed in the flat lands of your mid-west, Doctor. Millions and millions of years of dominance ceasing to exist in what was no more than a few ticks of the astronomical clock."

After a long pause, Leo continued. "The grids were set up so that all warriors were herding the Neanderthal toward a far point on their grid, a point that coincided with other points. It was an attempt to bring massive numbers of the enemy into a central location where there would be nowhere for them to flee. From accounts I have read, that plan actually worked in a few instances. But it looks like when it didn't, it was because one or more of the warriors were no longer hunting the Neanderthal."

"Do you mean some of your terminators developed a

167

conscience?" I said with a smirk. "Maybe, didn't have the stomach for so much blood shed? All those poor dead humans and animals rotting in the fields. Have you ever heard of Wyatt Earp, Leo?"

"Of course. Actually met him."

"Of course you did. Well, old Wyatt used to hunt buffalo. Hunting may not be the correct term. Wyatt used to shoot buffalo. Just as many as he could. And it wasn't hard. The poor dumb creatures just stood there grazing while their buddies were dropping like flies all around them. Anyway, it was a pretty lucrative gig for a while, but eventually he just couldn't do it anymore. He said the killing of the dumb beast and the stench of their rotting bodies after the hide had been ripped from it, just got to be too much. So he went and became a lawman. Do you think some of your boys may have just gotten sick of the killing? Is that what happened?"

"Unfortunately, no," said Leo. "It appears that some of them decided that rather than kill the Neanderthal they would use them instead. Obviously, it would not have been very difficult to get the caveman to follow them into battles. What soldier wouldn't want to carry their spear behind an advanced weapon wielded by a true professional?"

"Are you telling me," I said, laughing at the absurdity of it, "that instead of killing the cavemen so that Cro could prosper, they were organizing armies so they could kill Cro Magnon? The very people they were suppose to defend."

"So it would appear," said Leopold Christ, frowning at my enjoyment of that little tidbit.

ten

They moved warily toward one another, their weapon clutched tightly behind their backs, prepared to engage at the slightest movement of aggression from the other. The day was cold and dismal, a light snow falling, their footsteps leaving imprints in the accumulation on the yellowed grass. There were ten paces distance between them when they came to a stop. Neither spoke as they took the measure of the other. And then one of the men narrowed his blue eyes.

"You decided to grow a beard," he said. "Do you think it looks good on you, Petah?"

"It covers up the sagging skin, old friend. And now that I see you, I think that is a good thing. I think you should grow one, too, Alis. You might not look so old if you did."

"I don't mind looking like an old man, Petah. I just wish I didn't feel like one."

They stood staring at each other, their weapons ready. Finally, Alis said, "Even after all these years, I still marvel at this white moisture that falls on this planet. There is something comforting about it."

"Well, I don't like it. Having to wear these disgusting animal skins for warmth is not to my liking. Never has been. There is not enough warm days here like there was back home. I miss that."

"After all these years," said Alis, "I can barely remember home." Then his eyes narrowed once more. "Are we enemies now, Petah? Are you one of them?"

Very slowly, Petah brought his hand away from behind him, bent over and placed his weapon on the ground. And then he stood erect once more.

"What makes you think I am not one of the rogue ones?" Alis asked, bringing his weapon out in front of him.

"Of us all," said Petah, "you are the one who would never disobey orders. As you see, I have bet my life on that."

"Was I really so predictable?" asked Alis. "How

171

boring of me."

"Not boring, old friend. Comforting. I was always confident going into battle with you. Confident I would return safely. Now, do you have a shelter near here where we can get out of this damn cold?"

Alis laughed. "Yes, not too far. Do you have family with you?"

"No," Petah said with a sad shake of the head. "Only me. My sons are scattered across this land doing what they were taught to do. I had two daughters, but they were killed by the animals we seek to destroy. Brutally raped."

"I'm sorry, Petah"

"Many years ago now," Petah said. "They were avenged."

"What of Leda?" Alis asked.

"She, too, is dead. An illness. She was a good woman, Alis. And what of you? Does Ethra still live?"

"She does," said Alis, as he bent down to pick up Petah's weapon, and, handing it to him, said, "She will be happy to see you again. Come, I have built a shelter just beyond that grove of trees. You must be hungry."

"Oh, I eat well," he said rubbing his protruding belly, "but I certainly would not refuse a meal prepared by someone else."

They walked side by side through the gentle snow into the grove. "In the warmer months these trees are heavily weighted with a fruit that is quite delicious," Alis said. "Pale green on the outside and white flesh inside that is juicy and sweet."

Just beyond the grove was the shelter. Pulling back the animal hide, the two men stepped into the spacious interior. Ethra knelt by the fire pit, slowly turning a spit that held a large slab of meat. She looked up when they entered, her pale blue eyes squinting to better focus on the two men.

"You see, Alis," said Ethra, "how much more handsome a man you would be if you grew a beard. Look how young Petah still looks. Like the man who came to this world so many years ago. No different."

Petah laughed while Alis shook his head.

"As you can tell, my mate has eyes that are failing," Alis said.

"Yes, that is rather obvious," Petah said, laughing again.

173

"My eyes, however, are as good as ever, and they tell me, Ethra, that you are still quite a beautiful woman. How is it you have not aged a day in all these years?"

She stood and came to him, taking his hands in hers and looking into his eyes. "You see, Alis," she said, "this is how you talk to a woman. You tell her things she wants to hear. Petah was always so good at that. Do you remember? How you could turn a head, dear Petah. Many were jealous when Leda was chosen to come here with you."

"But I never could turn your head, could I Ethra?"

She smiled. "Perhaps if there had been no Alis....."

"Are you two done?" Alis said, taking a seat near the fire.

Ethra laughed, and returned to the cooking of the meat while Petah sat on the ground near Alis.

"Is Leda near here," Ethra asked. "I would so like to see her again. We had such fun when we were young."

Petah then told his two old friends about the long years since coming to the planet. The battles fought, the children born, the long illness of his mate. Alis realized, when Petah spoke of the many tribes he had battled, that Petah had had a

174

more difficult journey than he. He wondered if the others were finding as many battles to fight and enemy to kill as Petah had. They had been told to expect large numbers of the enemy that needed to be killed, but no one, during all their briefings, had even hinted at the actual numbers they would encounter. As young men, they had been trained to quell dissident factions. Small rebel forces that maybe numbered several hundred. But what they had been doing for the past ninety years they had been on this planet, Alis knew, went far beyond what they had trained for. To Alis, it felt more like they were assassins rather than soldiers. It seemed now like a senseless killing of a people that did not possess the weapons to even fight back, unlike back home where the rebels were armed with sophisticated weapons. He wondered, would it not have been better to demonstrate to the slant heads the uselessness of resistance and then at least give them the chance to live in peace? But he did not make policy. That was not his job. His was to execute the orders given, which he had been doing to the best of his ability ever since he was thirteen.

"So, like you, I have worked through my sector until

finally coming here, waiting for you and the others to arrive," Petah concluded. "I have been here almost ten years waiting."

Ethra had cut long slices of the meat and they ate while Alis recounted the history of their journey from the valley where he and Ethra had started, to where they now sat. Petah sat quietly eating and nodding, only interrupting when the tale recounted the time spent on the shores of the ocean.

"And you lived by this ocean?" he asked.

"For many years," Ethra said. "It was wonderful. You cannot imagine how wonderful. We would fall asleep to the rhythmic sound of the water lapping at the rocks and wake to that sound. I would walk through the cold water in the morning and bathe in it. It had a salty taste to it. Not like a river or lake. And there were waves of water that rose above the level of the water and they would have foam on top sometimes. Sometimes these waves rose to such a height that they could knock you over as they raced to the sand. And the fish would swim between my legs and nibble at my toes." She smiled. "I even taught myself to swim and float. Alis could not master it, but I did. It was a very happy time

176

for us. And the others were there. They stayed away from us, but I would sometimes catch them peeking at us from the cliffs. It was where we left our youngest daughter when we moved on. Six sons and two daughters. But now it is just us."

Petah finished the meat, licking his fingers and wiping them on the front of his wrap. "In the ten years I have been here, after destroying the tribe that had settled this area, I have been waiting for the migration of tribes that should have been fleeing the sectors between our two. I have not seen that happen. The question now becomes, has the enemy already come through here before I arrived, or have they all been wiped out so that there are none to come?"

Alis, cutting off another small slice of meat at the fire, said, "Or there could be another reason. Several years ago, I received a communique that said some of us had gone rogue. That some of us had abandoned the mission. It did not say who or why, only that they had."

"I received the same message," Petah said. "You would have thought they would have told us who. Or what they had done. I sent a message back asking for more

177

information, but I have received no further contact. It's almost like we are on our own, Alis."

"We may very well be," Alis said. "Ninety years we have been on this mission. My guess is, the council, or whoever is on the council now, believes we have done a good enough job and that our objective has been successful. Whatever happens now will be of little consequence to the grand scheme of things. Who knows how many of us are left. Certainly in the next fifty or sixty years none of us will still be alive. I'm sure it is the council's hope that our children will carry on with the plan, and their children after them, but I don't think that was really a major concern for them."

"You don't?" Petah asked.

"No. I never did. I have always thought that all the council cared about was that we kill as many of the slant heads as we could. Knowing how many tribes I have killed, and listening to what you have said about the battles you have waged, and only imagining how much death the others have probably caused, it would be my guess that the weaker ones will have no problem winning the planet now. That was

178

the real objective all along."

"You always had more of a feel for the political angle of what we did," Petah said with a shrug. "Me, I was just there for the action. But even I, after all these years, wonder about the necessity of all this death."

After a pause in the conversation, Petah asked, while staring into the fire, "You knew the men who came here, Alis. Who would you suspect of being the ones who went rogue?"

Shaking his head slightly, Alis replied, "I wouldn't even want to venture a guess. It would depend on what it was they have done. So many variables. Did some of them decide that it was too much effort to continue with the mission? Maybe. I remember being surprised when I saw some of the names of those chosen. They were not men I would have picked to be in a situation where they would have to think for themselves. Great at following orders, but not too bright if left to their own devices. A few of the names I saw concerned me. We are soldiers, Petah. It is our job, our duty, to carry out the orders we are given, and often those orders force us to kill. Most of us take no enjoyment in the killing. But some of the men who came here did enjoy the killing. Men like Lasser. Killing the slant heads or killing the others, I think, would matter not to them. Who knows?

"What I do know is, we are almost at the end of our mission. This old body is telling me there are very few battles left in it."

"Have you gone back to any of the places you have been?" asked Petah. "Checked to see how your children have fared with the surviving tribes?"

"We have not," said Ethra. "Not yet. But we are going to do that. It will be good to see the children again. They will all be grown. Probably with mates. I wonder if the council had taken that situation into consideration? We will do it as we journey back to the valley where we started."

"Going back to the beginning?" said Petah. "Now that is interesting. I would have thought you would go back to the ocean, you spoke so well of it."

"We thought about that," said Alis.

"But I loved the valley where we had our first two children," Ethra interrupted. "I would like to spend the rest of our lives there."

"I believe I will live out my remaining years right

here," Petah said. "Oh, I complain about the cold and the weather, but there are nights when the sky is alive with dancing lights and the wind whistles through the forests making a sound that is musical. As good a place as any to spend eternity and probably better than most."

They sat and talked and ate into the late evening, until Petah drifted off to sleep in front of the fire.

^   ^

Petah abandoned the shelter he had built and made another next to Alis and Ethra. The men hunted and fished during the day and reminisced for hours next to fires that lit the night. After two years of peaceful living, Alis decided it was time to begin the trek back to the valley from where they had started.

"We will be leaving in the next few days, Petah," Alis said. "Are you sure you don't want to come with us? Why spend the rest of your life alone?"

They stood thigh deep in the river, a short spear in their hands poised above the surface of the water, prepared to stab at any fish that ventured by.

"I have considered it quite a lot the last few days, but I am content here," Petah said. "But I thank you for the offer.

181

I will miss you two."

Petah stabbed at a fish, but missed. He cursed at his slow response.

"If our survival depended on your fishing ability we would all starve," Alis said with a laugh.

"And how many have you caught this morning?" asked Petah, glancing at the bank behind them. "There seems to be only rocks behind you."

"I never claimed I was good at catching fish," said Alis. "Only that I was better than you."

As Petah was about to scoff at that claim, Alis suddenly lifted his arm. "Listen," he said.

After a few moments, Petah said, "I don't hear anything."

Alis leaned back towards the bank of the river, straining his head higher, eyes closed. Then he began to climb the bank.

"It's Ethra," he said. "She's in distress."

Petah climbed the bank and began to follow his old friend who had broken into a run towards their shelter. Nearing the grove of trees, he could hear the calls of the

182

woman. Entering the grove, he saw Alis kneeling on the ground beside Ethra who laid prone on the sparse grass.

"Is she hurt?" Petah asked, coming up to them.

"It's my leg," said Ethra in obvious pain. "I fell out of the tree. How stupid of me."

"What are you doing climbing trees?" Petah asked, shaking his head. "Do you think we are still young and swinging on the vines in the Crellis jungle?"

"No. I was picking the fruit and reached for a nice fat one. I just misjudged the distance and ended up leaning too far. So ridiculous."

Alis had his device out and was scanning Ethra's leg. "Looks like a cracked bone. You won't be climbing any trees for a while. Let's get her back to the shelter, Petah."

Alis lifted her up and carried Ethra to their home. Laying her on a soft bed of hides, he then went out to find pieces of wood that he could use to make a splint. When that was done, the two men sat outside the shelter and spoke softly while Ethra slept.

"The injury will heal," Alis said, "but we won't be leaving anytime soon. She won't heal before the cold season begins, so it appears we will be here another year."

Nodding his head, Petah said, "Well, we will make her as comfortable as we can. Fortunately for you, I am a very good cook."

That got a laugh from Alis. "You cook like you fish, old friend, but if it saves me from doing it I will agree with you."

^   ^

The season of cold and white moisture seemed to Petah to have lasted longer than usual, but the ground was now clear and grass was beginning to green again. He was sitting with his two old friends outside of their shelter, sipping from a wooden cup a pleasant beverage made from minty leaves.

"You will be leaving soon?" he asked.

"Yes," said Alis. "You should come with us. The valley we return too gets cold weather, but nothing like this place and certainly not for as long. I'm telling you, you would like it there."

"I'm sure I would. Ethra, are you ready for such a long journey?"

"Ready or not, it is time for us to go. The leg feels

184

strong enough and I have gotten use to the limp. I do wish you would come with us, Petah. Why stay here alone?"

Petah shrugged. "You know, lately I have been having dreams about home. I wonder what our life would have been like if we had never come to this place. Do you ever wonder about that, Alis?"

"I wonder about a lot of things," Alis said with a smile. "None of which do me any good. What has been done cannot be undone. Our fate was sealed the day we were born. The best we could do was make the best of it. I have no regrets."

"Anyone want more tea?" Ethra asked as she slowly came to her feet.

Both men shook their heads as she limped into the shelter.

"Do you think she can make the trek?" asked Petah.

"We will go slow," Alis said. "There will be no need to rush."

Staring off into the grove of trees, Petah said, "I have been having other dreams, too. Not so pleasant as the ones about home."

He looked at Alis who was looking at him.

185

"In these dreams, I see the faces of the children. The countless ones I have killed over all these years. What was all this killing for, Alis? Why were we sent here to do this? Did it ever bother you? The killing of the children?"

Frowning, Alis said, "Of course. If it eases you any, you must realize that the children, once the parents were dead, would be defenseless in this world that punishes the weak. How long would they have lived before becoming the prey of an animal? How horrible would that death have been? As terrible as the killing of children was, it was an act of mercy. And as far as why we were sent here to kill one group of people and allow another group to live, I have no answer for that. No one ever told me. Maybe they didn't even know. Our leaders didn't always know what the council was thinking or why things were done."

He smiled at his old friend. "Petah, don't do this to yourself. What is done, is done. Let it go."

Ethra came back out with more tea and a hide to keep her warm. The three watched the sun setting over a distant mountain range that was still white from the cold season.

^   ^

His eyes snapped open. Ethra was already awake, warming water for her morning cup of tea. She hummed softly to herself and pulled the animal skin more tightly about her bare shoulders. Alis closed his eyes once more and listened. He shut out the sound of his mate's humming and concentrated his senses on another sound, a disturbance of the air from somewhere beyond the space where they lived. And he heard it again, the sound that had awakened him. It was a low rumble. Distinct. Almost rhythmic in its cadence. It stirred a memory in him from his youth, but it was a memory he could not quite grasp. Placing a hand on the ground, he felt just the slightest of a vibration tingling his fingertips.

Alis sat up on the skins and quickly slid one over him. Ethra saw him and smiled a good morning, but her smile quickly faded when she saw the look on his face. Before she could ask what the problem was, he was moving through the opening. Petah was walking towards him.

"Any idea what it is?" Petah asked.

Alis shook his head and began walking toward the grove of fruit trees. Ethra stepped out into the cool of the morning and asked what was the matter. He didn't reply.

Coming through the trees, the noise was louder now and the two men looked at each other. They knew what the rumble was. They could feel the vibration under their feet. Reaching the far edge of the grove, the expanse of grassland stretched before them in a long, gradual down hill slope that ran to the river far below them. Coming up the hill were slant heads. Thousands of them. Moving not as they usually did in a haphazard manner, but moving as one like a military march, their feet pounding the ground in unison. And in front of them, sitting atop a four legged white beast, rode a warrior, his body covered in the heavy skin of a bear.

"Do you believe this?" asked Petah.

"No," Alis replied. "I guess this is what was meant by rogue."

"Do you recognize who it is?"

"I'm not sure," said Alis. "It may be Flethar. He and his mate left the ship the stop before Ethra and me. I never trusted him. I always felt there was something going on in that brain of his that was just a little devious."

Petah tapped Alis on the arm and pointed to the far end of the hill to their left where another group of slant heads

188

were just coming into view marching up the hill toward them, also being led by a warrior riding a beast.

"Seems Flethar has an ally," said Petah.

Alis nodded. "Must be his brother Veryn. Remember what those two did in Chadron? They should have been disciplined for that, but the report was buried and the council never saw it."

"What do you think they are doing now? With this army they are leading."

"Maybe they are planning on conquering this world and claiming it for themselves," Alis said. "You know the two of them were never very smart."

"You have a plan?" asked Petah.

"No idea at all," Alis said as he stepped out of the grove and walked out into the tall grass of the field and stood there waiting for the hordes to approach. Petah came and stood beside him.

As the thousands of Neanderthals continued the assent up the grassy slope, Petah moved a distance away from Alis to face the horde approaching from the west. As he did, he noticed another horde that stood higher up the hill silently

189

watching the approaching mass. In front of them, another warrior sat naked atop a black beast.

"Alis," Petah called out loudly to be heard above the increasing noise of the marching army. He lifted his chin toward the stationary horde when Alis looked at him.

After a few moments, Alis said, "Lasser," then turned his attention back to the horde following Flethar.

'Lasser', thought Petah. 'I should have killed that maggot.' Then cursed himself for not having killed the maggot when he had insulted Leda one night in Chadron.

When the two approaching hordes got an equal distance from the two warriors who stood in the field, Lasser began to close the distance, slowly advancing down the hill. Alis waited patiently. Petah waited, too. He would take his cue from Alis.

At a distance where his voice could be heard by the approaching warriors, Alis raised his weapon and pointed it at Flethar. Petah did the same, pointing his at Veryn. The warrior brothers both pulled their beasts to a halt. The armies of slant heads behind them also came to an immediate stop. Lasser signaled his group to a stop. There was much

190

agitation in the groups. All of them knew the power of the shiny weapons.

For many minutes they stood like that, the three hordes facing the two warriors, the tension rising among the slant heads, eventually causing them to be quiet in anticipation of what their leaders would do.

"Alis, is that you?" Flethar called across the field as he leaned forward on his beast. "I can't believe you are still here. Shouldn't you be chasing the slant heads towards the ice? Have you gotten so old that you need to rest?" Flethar laughed. Then, "and who is that old man with you? Petah, is that you behind those whiskers? Do you remember the fun we had in Chadron, Petah? Those were the days, old friend."

Rising higher on the beast, Flethar slowly gazed across the width of the slope, his arm making a sweeping gesture.

"Isn't this a beautiful planet? I think I like it better than home. What about you, Alis? Do you long for the fields of Marliss or the jungles of Crellis? I remember you were always such a good little soldier, always telling us how lucky we were to be fighting against the rebels who wanted to destroy our way of life. We were always to obey the council,

191

because they knew what was best for everyone. Do you still feel that way? After all these years of killing the slant heads? Do you still feel that way? And why do you point your weapon at me, old friend? I am not your enemy."

"Flethar, you have not changed," said Alis. "The words that escape your mouth have no meaning, nor do they convey your intentions. Why do you and your brother lead an army of slant heads, when your orders were to kill them?"

"I did kill them," Flethar said. "Killed them for many years. Left the land safe for those who look like us. Then I started asking myself, why? What have the slant heads ever done to us, Alis? Why were they my enemy? Of course, the answer to that is, they are not my enemy. No reason for them to be. They are not your enemy either. So if they are not our enemy, why could they not be our ally?"

Again he swept his hand across the scope of the land and Alis saw he now held his weapon in the hand. "Why are we risking our lives for others, when all this can be ours? Have you ever considered that? Have you ever considered that if we all band together we can rule this planet and the council be damned? And there is nothing they can do about it."

"I see Veryn and Lasser follow your lead," Alis said, keeping his weapon pointed at Flethar atop the magnificent white beast. "Any of the others decide to join you?"

Flethar leveled his weapon, bringing it in line with the figure standing before him in the tall grass. "Several others," Flethar said. "Those who could see the wisdom in ruling the slant heads rather than purging them.

"They really are a simple people, are they not? Fearless in battle against the others, but absolutely petrified by the power of this," Flethar said, indicating his weapon with a slight flick of the wrist. "Such simple minds to bend to our will."

"And where are you going with this army that follows you?" Alis asked.

"Actually, we were coming here," Flethar said. "This area is the convergence of the five sectors. Here we would gather more allies to join us, or eliminate any who oppose us."

"And then what, Flethar? Have you thought it through?" Petah yelled across the field, never taking his eyes off Veryn, nor lowering the aim of his weapon.

"Of course I have, old friend," Flethar yelled back. "From here, we sweep east across the vast land, destroying all who oppose us and eventually meeting up with the others on the far side of the ice mass."

"And when the council sends troops to defeat you, what then?" Alis said.

Flethar shrugged. "By then, we will all be old or dead. In the meantime, we live like kings. Revered as gods by the simpletons who we command. Now, will you join us, Alis?"

"Join you?"

"Of course," Flethar said. "We were comrades once. Played together as children. Do you forget, old friend? I have no wish to kill you. Join us and we will rule this planet. The choice is simple. Join us or die."

After many moments of hesitation, Flethar then said, "You are surrounded, Alis. Even if you manage to slay me before I slay you, Lasser will cut you and Petah down. It is hopeless. You were always the wisest among us. Be wise now."

Alis looked across the scope of the hill that was covered with thousands of slant heads, their faces lifted in defiance, flat noses breathing heavily, spears and newly constructed axes at the ready. He realized Petah and he did not have a chance against three warriors and the armies they commanded.

"I believe I prefer death to an alliance with you," Alis' voice echoed across the fields.

"So be it!" Flethar yelled across the field as his weapon suddenly leveled at Alis. But nothing happened. Flethar looked down at his hand and then back at Alis. Veryn and Lasser were also looking down at their weapons.

"What do you think?" Petah said to Alis, as he looked back and forth between Veryn and Lasser who sat upon their beasts shaking their weapons and re-aiming.

In response, a bolt blasted across the distance, ripping a hole through the bear skin and sending Flethar off the beast to land among the throng behind him. Petah then blasted the naked body of Lasser, the bolt exploding through the man's muscled chest. Veryn screamed out a curse and coaxed his beast into a charge at the two warriors who both then turned their weapons toward him and blasted him and his beast, sending them sideways into a tumble that left them in a mangled heap upon the ground.

The hill became deathly silent when the echoes of the blasts died down. Petah and Alis stood in a crouch, their weapons aimed at the horde of slant heads. The Neanderthals stood in shock at the swiftness of the death of their leaders. And then mayhem.

Thousands of slant heads came charging at the two warriors from all three directions. Just as many began running in the opposite directions, their fear of the powerful weapons overcoming their natural aggression.

Alis and Petah began swinging their weapons in widening arcs as they began backing up toward the grove, seeking shelter from the spears that rained towards them thrown by the advancing mass. Dismembered bodies slammed onto the ground only to be stepped on or over by the mass that kept advancing. The grunting and yelling was deafening, as was the pounding of the feet on the ground by the rampaging horde. Alis concentrated his beam on the army that had followed Flethar, that being the largest of the three. Petah kept up a steady attack on the slant heads that were racing down the hill. They would reach him before

Veryn's group would.

The two warriors reached the grove, seeking shelter behind the trees from the constant barrage of spears that were hurled at them. Alis heard a groan from Petah and, looking over at his old friend, saw he had a spear in his thigh. Petah broke the shaft and stepped behind a tree. Alis stepped back into the field and sent the powerful beam across the front line of Veryn's charging group, sending arms, legs and heads tumbling to the ground and the intensity and speed with which this happened caused those behind them to slow their advance. Alis then swung his weapon toward the uphill charge of Flethar's horde and then he charged at them, staying close to the treeline, his beam cutting down the enemy like a scythe through grass. As spears rained down around him, he moved rapidly, needing to get to the beginning of the grove before the horde did or they would flank him and have the advantage of cover. This maneuver seemed to confuse them, and the Neanderthals swept toward the middle of the hill rather than the safety of the grove where they had intended on going. They were now out in the open and defenseless against the power of the beam.

Petah propped himself against a tree and concentrated his beam on Lasser's group, seeing that Alis had slowed the advance of Veryn's horde. Petah kept his arc narrow and the bodies piled up in that space. The slant heads charging down the hill saw the pile of bodies and began moving towards them, hoping to use the dead as a shield. It was what Petah had hoped for, giving him a chance to move towards a spot where he could keep the horde from entering the trees to his left where they would have the advantage on him. Another spear grazed his shoulder as he moved. He hardly noticed. Blood was pouring freely from the wound in his leg.

Alis had kept the horde from entering the southern part of the treeline, and he now pressed the attack, his beam inflicting incredible carnage. It was having an effect on the enemy. The charge was losing steam and the horde began retreating, with many of them in full run down the hill. The slant heads in the rear of Veryn's army, witnessing the panic retreat of the others, also began to flee. Constantly moving left, Alis came upon the front guard of Veryn's horde and he let loose with an arc that encompassed both Veryn's group and the last of Flethar's army who had not yet retreated.

Body parts were flung high into the air from the power of the beam that grew in intensity from the adrenaline surging through the body of Alis and the hill was red with blood, the air vibrating from the crying and screams of the dying and the heated air the weapons caused. Those still advancing soon found it impossible to step forward without stepping on a dismembered leg, arm, head, and their resolve quickly faded and they joined the others in retreat.

Alis moved quickly back into the grove and raced to where Petah was resting against a tree awaiting another charge from the remaining slant heads from Lasser's army.

"Let me put a tourniquet on that," Alis said, indicating the blood soaked leg.

"No time for that," said Petah. "Here they come."

The charge came at a frenzied, chaotic rush, the Neanderthals leaving the shield of the dead, hurtling the short distance toward the tree line. But they had not expected the second warrior to be there with the wounded one, and the two tall men stood at the northern entrance to the grove and executed the maneuver that they had been taught almost a hundred years before. It was all over very quickly after that.

199

The enemy had gotten dangerously near the entrance, but could not breach it as the dead piled up. Finally, they stopped trying to enter the grove and began running past it in retreat down the hill, following the others. Alis came out of the grove behind them, his weapon arcing across the fleeing horde, dropping them to die among the countless dead already littering the hill.

He surveyed the field and saw no enemy who still stood, then he turned to go back to Petah. Ethra was already with him, working to stop the bleeding which was gushing, Petah having pushed the spear head through his leg so he could maneuver better. She was attempting to rip her hide so she could wrap the wound when Petah gently took her hand in his.

"Ethra," Petah said, smiling, "sit beside me. There is nothing you can do. Look, here comes Alis. Not a scratch on him. He is like a god. Look how he walks. Hundreds of the enemy dead and not a scratch on him. What an honor it is to go into battle with such a man."

Alis came up to them and looked down at his old friend. He saw the wound and the tremendous amount of blood that flowed from it soaking the ground. He saw the look on his mate's face.

"We have defeated them, Petah," Alis said. "Just like the old days at Chadron. They ran from us with fear in their eyes. And those too foolish to run are dead. Two old men, who should be sitting in rocking chairs and telling stories of old battles to their grandchildren. Yet here we are creating legends."

Petah reached up and took Alis' hand. "Thank you, old friend," he said. "I feared I would die in my bed, alone and bored." Petah smiled. "It has never been boring when you are around, Alis. Thank you, my friend. This is the way a warrior should die."

With Ethra holding his left hand and Alis holding his right, Petah began to sing an old drinking song that was popular when they were all very young and a life of adventure was ahead of them. After the third line, he became silent and his head dipped forward and the blood stopped pulsing from the wound. Ethra lifted his hand and kissed it, then slumped back against the tree. Alis looked out to the top of the hill and the mountain that rose beyond it. He would

201

find a spot up there to bury Petah. A spot that faced to the north and the lights that danced upon the night time sky.

eleven

Shaking my head slightly, I looked past Leo, up to a bright sun that shone from the middle of a baby blue sky. "So, not everything went according to Hoyle," I said. "What a shame. Any other problems our poor giants had that you might know about?"

Leo shrugged. "Overall, the warriors time here was considered a success by the council. The Neanderthal tribes became extinct. Most of the tribes of man were beginning to make significant progress in their advancement as they learned to farm and communicate from the generations of the warriors children who showed them the way. Over time, the great grandchildren of the warriors assimilated into the tribes and their job was done. There was no more they could teach because there was no more that they knew. There was more progress made in the next two thousand years than had been made in all the million years before. Man was finally on the path to creating a society."

"Left to our own devices, man did alright," I said. For some reason, I felt the need to defend us. No idea why. It was all utter nonsense. I look at my watch. As I sit here, I am trying not to lose sight that Leo has offered to finance three more digs. I do not want to jeopardize that financing, but I am growing quite weary of Leopold Christ. I should just get up and go, but I am curious as to why he has gone through such an elaborate ruse. What is his end game?

"Leo, you mentioned there was a reason you were sent here," I said. "And others before you. What is that all about? Neanderthals were gone. Man was progressing. Why were others sent?"

"Because time is not infinite, Daniel, despite what you may believe. Especially, when there is a ticking bomb right beside you. Yes, the people of Earth were making strides

204

during the next few thousand years. Unfortunately, they were baby steps. From the correspondence of the time that I was allowed to read, there were several members of the various councils who advocated that Earth should be allowed to progress at whatever pace they could, regardless of how slow it may seem. There were some who felt it made no difference whether we came to a world with huge cities or simply small villages. Either way, it would be an inferior world.

"But there were others who felt it would be a very difficult hardship on those who came if there was no modernization beyond ox carts and water holes. So, my dear Doctor Reynolds, over the years Eden has sent individuals who helped prod things along."

"Prod things along?"

Leo shrugged. "Quite often, too, I must say. Among the people of Earth, there always seemed to be a reluctance to change. You have no idea, Daniel. It is my understanding that the concept of cities, Damascus and Jericho in particular, was not met with enthusiasm initially. A descendant of one of the warriors had somehow managed to unite enough tribes

205

together to raise the city of Aleppo, but no one else had success in that endeavor. At least not until Jericho several thousand years later. The success of Jericho was a stepping stone in progress and the wall was a major reason for it. That was us, Daniel. The idea for it. The safety we knew it would convey to all who saw it. But even then it was a tough sell."

"And why was that?"

Leo shrugged. "Perhaps because of all the years of turmoil with the Neanderthal. Tribes may have been reluctant to join together to become another entity. Obviously, language would have been a huge barrier. The warrior children were tasked with teaching our language to the tribes they encountered, but over two or three thousand years who knows how much that would have changed in the passing down of the language."

"Are there different languages on Eden?" I ask. I find myself trying to think of ways to catch Christ in a lie, or at least a moment of hesitation.

"Obviously, there was," he said, "way back when. Dozens if not hundreds. But the early councils decreed that the planet would only have one common language. It took

206

two thousand years, but it finally happened. It is a difficult thing to erase a culture. Especially ones that have been in existence for forty thousand years."

"I will assume the official language of Eden is not English," I said.

Leopold Christ smiled. "No, my dear friend, it is not."

"Is your language spoken anywhere here on this planet still, taught to us, as you claim, by the children of warriors?"

"There is a tribe, in the bush of Nigeria, who speak many of our words, but I know of nowhere else."

"Well, what will happen when Edenites come in the future? Will all of Earth need to learn their language or will they be able to communicate with us using their superior intellect? Did you learn English on Eden before coming here, Leo, or did you pick it up once you got here?"

"Actually, I had a passing knowledge of French and Russian before coming here. Since then, I have mastered German, English, Italian, Japanese and Cantonese."

"Impressive," I said with a nod. "Erwarten sie wirklich, das ich all dies glaube?"

Again that hideous smile, "Welchen Grund hatte ich,

207

Daniel, fur eine solche Erfindung?"

"Je n'en ai aucune idee et c'est ce qui m'inquiete," I replied, my French a little less rusty than my German. Madeline and I had conversed often in her native tongue. Deiter had less patience with me.

"Ease your concerns, my dear friend," Leo said to me, his eyes less intense than usual. "I have no reason to lie to you. All I tell you is true."

"Well, is it true aliens built the Great Pyramids?" I asked, leaning forward in the chair and raising my eyebrows. "What about Easter Island? Surely, they created Stonehenge?"

He frowned. "Can we please be serious, Daniel? There are things that need to be done and I do not have much time left?"

"You have mentioned that several times," I said. "Why is that? Are you dying? You claim to be an old man, and clearly you are, but just how old are you, Leopold Christ? Or should I ask how long ago you came to Earth?"

Once more Leo walked to the open window and stood looking out toward the Mall. "I arrived here in the year of

1896 Earth time, beginning my career, I guess you would call it, in St. Petersburg. Thus the study of the Russian language. It was certainly an interesting time to be in Russia, Daniel, I must say. I was twenty-eight years of age. I was quite nervous, as you would expect, and totally unprepared for the culture shock this world presented. I was told about the primitive conditions here on Earth, even shown movies of it, but the reality of life here was quite depressing. I actually felt sorry for all those who had come before me to even worse conditions."

"Why Russia?" I asked.

"Good question. The man who was here before me had spent most of his years in England. But he had also spent many years in France and Russia. His suggestion was, the next one of us to come to Earth, should come to Russia. He felt that would be the place to be in the latter half of the nineteenth century."

"The place to be?" I said. "To do what? What exactly were you suppose to do? Why were you here?"

Leo turned from the window and looked at me. "For ten thousand years we have been coming to Earth," he said.

"And the reason has always been the same. We come to observe."

"Observe?"

"Yes," Christ said, nodding as he walked back to the chair. "Observe. When possible, ingratiate ourselves into circles of power. If we do, then the hope is we can then become an influential voice in the commerce of the country. Which is why we try to begin in countries that are powerful at the time or appear ready to begin strong economic growth. The gentleman I replaced came here in 1700. On advice from the person before him, who primarily had spent his time in Spain, he came to England. From all the communications he sent back to the council, it appears both men had had a tremendous amount of influence on the industrialization of Europe. The last communication received in 1864 suggested Russia appeared poised to become the great power of the second half of the 19th century."

"I think your council got some bad advice," I said with a chuckle.

With a shrug, Leo said, "Certainly by the time I arrived any chance they may have had at glory had passed them by. I observed for several years, but it was painfully obvious that a succession of wars, a failed agricultural plan, ineffective political policy and the general apathy of the populace, were all contributing to a country that held no promise of progress. The threat of war with Japan was the final straw, shall we say, and I left Russia for France in the Fall of 1904.

"Two years later, I read of the young American president who mediated the Treaty of Portsmouth that ended the Russian, Japanese War. That was Theodore Roosevelt. That got me interested in America. Interestingly, the last communication Eden had received mentioned the fledgling country that was mired in a civil war and it was suggested North America should be avoided, as should the land masses of Australia and Africa. But a lot had happened in America in forty years and after reading about Mr. Roosevelt, and understanding my time in Russia was not well spent, I came to America."

"When was that?" I asked.

"1907. On a steamship from France. I almost stayed in France, actually. Beautiful country, really. Quite civilized. Artistically cultured. They were making great strides in

211

science, too. Best of all, there were no cowboys. I had heard about your American West and had no passion to share those experiences. But, with a great sadness, I decided America might be the country that would lead the world in the new century, and off I went."

Leo leaned back into the cushions, his eyes dancing around the room. "Almost one hundred and twenty years ago, Daniel," he said. "So much has happened and yet it feels like it was yesterday. I remember standing on the deck of the ship as it cruised past the Statue of Liberty. Standing with all the other passengers on the crowded deck of that ship. We stood in total silence, looking up at the proud lady in the harbor. I was surrounded by all these poor people who had left their country looking for a better life. Some of them held their children. Some of them wore all that they owned. Many of them wept. I will tell you, my dear friend, that those were the most emotional moments of my life, standing on that deck and seeing what it meant to those people to be coming to America."

He looked at me then. "I think it was at that moment that I fully realized the importance of my mission. I had read the communications sent back to Eden by the others who came before me. All the way back to the Sumerians who learned to dry bricks in the sun, irrigate land and wheel a vehicle. Those who made their marks in Memphis and Thebes, Athens, Rome, Carthage, Madrid and London. The weight of it all, on that deck, was oppressive. The great city of New York, the greatest city in the world at that time, was before me, and all I saw was a backward society. Ages behind what I had left on Eden. But I also saw something else while I stood in that silent throng as we slowed into Ellis. I saw possibility. This was a country that offered possibility. This was a country that wanted to be great. This was a country where apathy did not exist and ideas were rewarded. This was a country where entrepreneurs could be found everywhere and all they needed for success was some financial assistance and maybe the seed of an idea to be planted in their brain. This was the country I needed to be in."

"A seed of an idea?" I said, with a shake of my head. "So, we have the great Leopold Christ, traveler from a distant galaxy, to thank for .... what? What great inventions?

213

LEOPOLD CHRIST

What marvels of modern science? Which men that we now revere achieved their greatness with the help of Leopold Christ?"

He looked across the room at me with that wrinkled face and I detected a flash of anger in those ancient eyes. Then his eyes softened and he said, "You mentioned Wyatt Earp."

I wasn't expecting that and I sighed. "You change subjects faster than a catcher changes signals to a pitcher. Why is it I can't get an answer from you, Leo?"

"But I am answering your queries, dear boy," Leo said, his eyebrows raised. "Just in my own way. I have had the opportunity to meet many of the most famous people of the last century. Scientists, politicians, inventors, masters of commerce. The movers and shakers, I believe is the term that is fancied now a days, who have shaped the modern world. I have contributed a great deal of money into many various political campaigns, funded quite a few entrepreneurial dreams, some of which I may have helped along with a thought or two. It matters not which ones. But of all the famous people I have had the opportunity to speak with, I found my dear friend Wyatt to be one of the more interesting."

"Your dear friend Wyatt?"

Leo shrugged.

"I met him on a movie set in Los Angeles in the early twenties. Of course it was a western movie, which, by the way, I became quite fond of. Remember I said the thought of cowboys repulsed me? Well, I became enamored of the genre after watching my first cowboy movie. It was exhilarating, Daniel, I must say. These rugged men wearing big hats, speeding through sagebrush on magnificent steeds, their six shooters blasting away the bad guys. All of it happening on a twelve foot high movie screen. So enjoyable.

"Wyatt and I had a such an enjoyable conversation that day. He was over seventy years old at the time, but still quite a man. Ramrod straight. Not much of a talker, but after a while of me doing most of the talking, he relaxed a bit and opened up a little. He regaled me with tales of his days in Dodge, Tombstone, the range. I could see the fire that still burned in his old eyes and could imagine the hesitancy those eyes would have produced in anyone facing him in a gun battle. There was an aura about him that suggested you were in the presence of a very dangerous man. I remember thinking, this must have been what it was like for anyone facing the warriors who quelled the revolts on Eden. I had the opportunity to speak with him several times over the next few years before he passed. He was quite a man."

I glanced at my watch. I had someone I wanted to speak with at the Smithsonian and would have the time to do it before dinner with my brother if I didn't waste anymore time with Leopold Christ and this ridiculous tale.

"I'm sure you have a hundred nostalgic stories you would love to share with me, but I don't have the time. Where are we going with all of this? I'm sorry, I don't believe any of it. I don't believe you came here from another planet. I don't believe the bones in those tombs did either. I don't believe the tale of a doomed planet."

Shaking my head, I placed the coke can on the side table and rose to leave. "What do you want, Leo? What the hell is this all about? It's the one question I keep asking and it is the one question you keep avoiding. What do you want?"

216

Leopold Christ leaned back into the cushions of the seat and looked up at me with those intense eyes. The little bit of color that had been on his cheeks earlier was now gone. "What I want, Daniel, is for you to believe what I am telling you. Obviously, I have failed. Let me ask you something, my young friend. How many tombs would it have taken for you to believe what I am telling you? How many to convince you? If we had had the time, how many would it have taken?"

"I could dig up a hundred such tombs," I said, walking over to where he sat, "but it would not change the one overwhelming evidence to dispute your story."

"And what is that?" Leo asked, his hands outspread.

"Their DNA is ours. They are man. Taller, yes. But they are man. Not some alien life form. That is tested. That is documented. That is truth. All you have given me is a story. I need more than that. When you decide to tell me the reason for all of this, I'll be happy to hear you out. But until then, I don't believe we have much more to say to each other. I'll let myself out."

"Will you be seeing your brother while you are here?"

217

LEOPOLD CHRIST

Leopold asked as I turned to leave.

Turning back to face the old man again, I said, "As a matter of fact, I am having dinner with him tonight. Why do you ask?"

"Perhaps," Leopold said, that smile again marring the wrinkled face, "you might mention our conversation to him."

"And why would I do that?" I said, narrowing my eyes, my voice rising. "This has no concern for him."

"Actually, Doctor Reynolds, it does. And it will. You should mention to your brother your thoughts on your discoveries. And you should mention our conversation today. It is important."

"If the President asks about the digs, and I am sure he will, I will enjoy telling him all about them. Just because he is my brother and he loves me, and cares about what I do for a living. But I see no reason to bring up this discussion. None at all. Good day, Mr. Christ." I turned and left the suite.

twelve

We sat across from each other on sofas in the residence. I was nursing my second seven and seven while Matthew sipped at a ginger ale. I had not seen my older brother in over a year, except on television, and he appeared to have aged ten years in that time. The lines on his forehead had doubled and deepened, the crow's feet at his eyes more pronounced. His voice was still strong, however, and he seemed to be in fine spirits. He mentioned getting some bill through the Senate earlier that day that he was happy about. Usually, when anyone talked politics, I faded out. When he was alive, my father and Matthew would have long discussions at the dinner table about the political climate of the time when we all got together for the holidays. Bored me out of my mind.

"Have you been down to visit mom?" Matthew asked.

"No," I said. "I called her when I got back from Brazil. She sounded good. Said she was having lunch with friends and asked if I could call back later."

"That's mom," Matthew said with a laugh. "You've been on an exciting dig and she's more concerned with the gossip going around the restaurants table. She'll never change."

"No, I don't suppose she ever will," I said. "I'm just happy she has friends she can socialize with. I worried she would go into a shell when dad died. Their circle of friends back home seemed to be his friends."

"Well, don't worry about mom," said Matthew with a shake of his head. "Her social calendar is full. I asked her to come up to Camp David over the Fourth for a nice visit. You know what she said?"

I shook my head.

"She said all the girls were getting together for a bus

220

trip over to the Hard Rock in Tampa and she didn't want to miss out."

"You're kidding?" I said. Matthew shook his head and laughed. Just then dinner was wheeled in and we moved to the table.

"So, tell me about Brazil," he said, as we started in on lamb shanks. "Your discoveries have created quite a stir."

I told him all about the digs in France and Brazil. The accidental sighting of the sarcophagus in the stone. The excitement of the find and the significance of finding what may be a previously unknown race of man. He listened with that look upon his face that said he was genuinely interested in what you were saying. It was a look that had served him well at countless house gatherings in his early political career.

"You believe these bones of giants are from the human race?" he asked after we retreated back to the sofas with coffee. He had lit up a thick cigar, the only vice I knew him to have.

"DNA tested," I said, "even though nothing like them have been unearthed before. I suppose they could have been a lone tribe of tall men and their kind died out with their death."

"But the two you have found are over five thousand miles apart and across an ocean. How do you explain that?"

I shrugged. "Right now, I can't. More research will be done. Somewhere, at sometime and somehow, someone will make a discovery that will make sense of it all. It's the way things happen. A discovery builds upon a past discovery and so on, and then logical conclusions are reached. Maybe when that happens this group of new human will be classified Danielthal. Or Homo Reynoldsectus."

Matthew laughed out loud. "Cute," he said. Then his face grew serious. "Have you considered that they may have come from another world?"

"Oh, lord," I said with a shake of my head. "Not you, too."

"This has been suggested to you?" Matthew asked.

I spent the next hour telling him about Leopold Christ. He didn't interrupt me once and I could see he was quite interested. When I finished, I looked at him and with narrowed eyes said, "You don't seriously believe in an alien

222

presence here on Earth, do you?"

Matthew leaned back into the cushions and re-lit the cigar, puffing away until he had a nice glow coming off the end of it. Then he looked at me, smiled and said, " Tell me more about this Leopold Christ. He sounds like quite a character."

"Oh, he is that," I said. "A disturbing little fellow. When we first met, I found his mannerisms and his way of talking rather quaint and I was put off by them. But he grew on me. But that only lasted for a little while. I find him tiresome and disturbing. I never seem to get a straight answer from the man. And now this nonsense that he is a traveler from another world who is a hundred and fifty years old and sent here to help speed us into great advances in progress."

"You believe none of that?"

"Come on, Matthew. It's ridiculous. From the first time I met him, I have had a disturbing feeling about the man."

"What kind of feeling?" Matthew asked, leaning forward on the sofa.

"I don't know," I said with a shrug and a slight shake of the head. "Hard to explain. It's like a feeling of impending

223

disaster." I laughed. "Maybe it's because he looks like a walking cadaver, but I have never felt comfortable around the man."

"There's something else, Danny," Matthew said. "What is it?"

"I don't know what he wants," I said softly. "I can't figure it out. He makes these wild claims and I don't know if it is dementia or some diabolic ploy of some kind."

"Diabolic ploy? To what end? What would be the purpose?"

"That's just it," I said. "What's his end game? Is he trying to disparage my career? Is he trying to embarrass you by embarrassing me? He has spent a lot of money on these digs. What's in it for him? I can't figure it out."

My brother fixed me with the famous Matthew Reynolds stare, his pale blue eyes penetrating right into my core. Then he smiled. "I received a call from your Mr. Leopold Christ this afternoon," he said.

I suppose I should be more surprised than I am, but things don't surprise me very much anymore since France. "You did?" I calmly said. "Did you speak with him?"

"We had a very pleasant conversation," Matthew said. Then, with a wave of the cigar, "Politicians find it advisable to speak with large donors when they call until large donors become a pain in the ass. Anyway, he had nothing but high praise for my younger brother. Must have said a hundred times how fond he was of his young friend Daniel. Proclaimed that you had made the most important archaeological discovery ever and that I must be incredibly proud of you."

"Did he happen to mention why it was so important?" I asked.

"No, he didn't," said Matthew. "Only that it was THE most important."

"Well, it's not," I said, "but he has said the same thing to me countless times. What did you think of him, Matt? Did he sound lucid to you or a rambling wreck?"

"He sounded quite lucid to me," Matthew said. "A bit over the top, to be sure, but he didn't sound crazy."

"Did he tell you about the bones and warriors and alien beings? Did he tell you he was an alien? Did he say he was from the planet Zorn here to steal our water supply?"

225

Matthew laughed. "Is that why he's here?" he said. "I should have guessed. No. Actually, he told me nothing beyond how pleased he was that you had found the bones. Really, he couldn't stop raving about you."

"Well, I think the old fella is crazy," I said with a frown. "I've decided I don't want anything else to do with him and I am not going to accept any more money from him for future digs. I think he's bad news."

Matthew shrugged. "You may want to sleep on that decision, Danny. Money now a days is getting hard to come by. Don't burn bridges. Anyway," he said, looking at his watch, "we need to call it a night. I'm leaving early in the morning for the coast and have some paperwork I need to review tonight.

"Listen," he said as we stood and walked toward the doors, "it's been great seeing you again. Been too long. I want you to come to Camp David over the Fourth. Spend a couple of days. Patty and the boys will be there and they are dying to see you. You won't believe how much Marty has grown. What do you say?"

"I have a ton of stuff to do...." I began to say when

226

Matthew suddenly reached over and took me into a headlock and started giving me a nooky.

"What's that you were saying, little brother? You would love to spend time with your family. Is that what I heard you say?"

"Okay, okay," I shouted into his side. "I'll come, I'll come."

"Good," he said, releasing me. "The kids will be excited. Come out Saturday morning. It'll be fun. And speaking of fun," he said as we walked down the stairs, "you look like you could use some. I hear there is a new bar in D.C. that all the young women are flocking to. The guard at the gate will tell you where it is."

"I'm fine," I said.

"Well, you don't look fine. Now get out of here," Matt said, giving me a hug. "I have work to do."

thirteen

The journey had not been difficult, but Ethra was pleased to have it done as she stood in front of the cave that had been their first home and looked out over the valley that hadn't changed at all in the past ninety-five summers, except for the crude huts that had been built along the tree line that bordered the valley, imitations of the one Alis had built so long ago. A soft rain was coating the vegetation and the various shades of green all shimmered with wetness. The bone she had broken in her leg in the fall from the tree ached slightly, as it always seemed to do on damp days. She was thankful Alis had captured the strange white beast Flethar had ridden into battle so she could sit atop it on the journey back.

Alis had found a spot in the mountain above the field of battle where he thought Petah would be pleased to spend eternity. While Alis had gone to work with his device creating a casket from the limestone, she had prepared the body of her old friend for the sacred ceremony given to all warriors of honor. She had removed all skin, muscle and organs from the body, placing everything atop a deer hide. She then used hot water to cleanse the bones completely clean. When she was done, Alis lit the hide on fire and recited the ancient words as the soft remains of Petah were consumed by the flames. The bones were then brought to the waiting casket, where Alis took great care in gently laying them in exact placement according to the old ways. When this was done, he then recited more of the ancient words, and then the two of them slipped the casket into its final resting place. Alis had taken her hand then and they had slowly walked back to their shelter.

That had been almost five years before. On their journey back to this valley, they had stopped at six of the sites they had been to over the years, the six sites where they had left their off-spring to teach man how to leave the caves. Four of her six children still survived and she was pleased they had all taken mates and had children of their own. Many children. And most of those children had taken mates and were having more children. Alis was pleased that where there had been tribes huddled in caves, fearful of the wrath of the slant heads, man now lived in communities of huts and cultivated the land. The plan the council had hoped would benefit this world seemed to be progressing.

They had spent one entire year at the ocean. Their youngest daughter had been left there many years before and Alis was pleased when he saw how much progress had been made by the people who lived there. The daughter had taught the people language. She also had shown them how to make a raft and how to catch fish in nets that she fashioned from the kelp. Ethra was pleased that her youngest had also found the time to have six children of her own and they were all fair haired and tall.

Their first son was now an old man and he had created a prosperous village of over one hundred huts situated in a massive circle around communal farmland. He, too, had taught language to the people. He had also taught fighting tactics to the men that had proven beneficial when they had been attacked by a tribe of slant heads. The Neanderthals had been defeated and peace had now been among them for many, many years. He had also begun trading the vegetables they grew with other tribes of men who resided two days from their village. These men had come to their village and had been curious about the construction of the huts, the tilling of the land. They were taught the way things were done and they had brought that knowledge back to their tribe. The son's village was a ten day walk from where Alis and Ethra would eventually live out their final days and Alis made sure his son, grandsons and great-grandsons would make that journey periodically. If he were to die before Ethra, he wanted to make sure she would be cared for. If she died before him, they were to finish the burial process.

When they had first returned, there was a great deal of curiosity from the inhabitants of the tribe who lived by the edge of the forest. Alis had gone into the settlement, but no one came out to greet him and no man came out to confront him. His days of killing were hopefully now over and he wanted to show these men skills that would make their lives easier. Alis had no way of knowing that in the cave across the valley on the other side of the mountain, a scene depicting a tall man standing in the center of many dead had been painted on the wall almost a century before by Drak.

"It is done," Alis said as he came out of the cave to stand beside his mate in the soft mist.

Ethra nodded, and then pushed that knowledge from her mind. Death would come soon enough. There was no need to think about it now. Below them she watched a black bear walk slowly across the valley, two cubs following close behind. She looked at Alis and he smiled. He took her hand and they slowly walked down the path that led to the flat grassland. The rain stopped as they walked and just as the sun broke through the clouds Alis came to a halt and pointed at a spot where the berry bushes grew in density and the land overlooked a stream.

"I will build our home there," he said. His plan was to build something more elaborate than they had been living in all these years, because they would not be leaving it.

Remembering the days she and her first daughter, who no longer lived, would bathe in the cold water of the stream and pick berries for their morning meal, Ethra nodded and smiled. They were home. They would journey no more.

fourteen

I pulled up to the guard shack and the marine on duty stepped out. Mark Sharpe followed the marine, and walked up to the passenger door.

"Can I hitch a ride up to the cabin?" asked Mark, the President's chief-of-staff.

I looked at the floor of the front seat and saw the fast food wrappers and empty cups from three days of being away from home.

"Sure, if you don't mind the mess," I said.

Sharpe opened the door and slid in to the Range Rover. "You call this a mess? This is nothing. I've been

234

campaigning for over 40 years and not always on some luxury bus. Hell, in the old days, there would be so much junk on the floor you couldn't see your feet."

The marine waved us through. "You spending the weekend, too?" I asked.

"Looks that way," Sharpe said. "There's a little tension going on right now between Pakistan and India, so we'll keep an eye on it. Might have a few visits from State tomorrow morning. We'll see. How have you been? Heard you had some amazing discoveries. You must be thrilled."

"It's like anything else now-a-days," I said with a shrug. "No matter what is discovered, no matter what is attained, someone is out there ready to tear it down. I pity the poor person who discovers the cure for cancer. Social media will tear them apart." I looked at Mark. He was looking out the side window.

"Patty and the boys here?" I asked.

"They're coming in late this afternoon," Mark Sharpe said. "They have been up at her parents place in Ogunquit since school got out. They are excited that you'll be here." Then he looked at me. "What did you think of Brazil?"

235

"You mean the dig?"

"No. The rain forest. I understand you were in an area that had been cleared."

"What's to think?" I said. "It's being destroyed day by day, mile by mile. Anyone with half a brain would be angry about what is going on there. So I'm angry. Can't anything be done about it?"

"Like what?" Mark asked. "We've made our views on this quite plain to the president of Brazil. He doesn't care what we think. Or anyone else, for that matter. It's their country and they will do what they want and the rest of the world can go to hell."

"Sanction them into submission," I said, probably a little more strenuous than was called for.

"That only hurts the people, and the people are poor enough as it is. The government is corrupt and could care less if the people are starving. They'll profit from the rape of the country and won't be around for the final act. Not much we can do short of backing a coup, but before we can do that we need to find someone honest down there who could gain the support to run the country."

"Nobody strong enough?" I asked.

Mark frowned. "Nobody honest enough."

I pulled up to the front entrance and another marine was there to greet us. I left the Rover running and he got in and took it to wherever the vehicles were parked. Mark led me up the stone stairs. I had never been to Camp David and was a little taken aback by the plainness of the building. I could understand why Eisenhower probably enjoyed the place, and Reagan, too. They were pretty level headed guys. But I could also see where the rest of the Presidents since Ike may not have thought the place to be ideal. The front entrance opened as we approached and there stood my brother with this big grin on his face. "Where did you pick this loner up, Mark?" he said, his arms reaching out to give me a bear hug.

"He seemed lost and hungry so I brought him here for a meal," Mark said. "Isn't that what we liberals do?"

"First, I think we'll give him a few beers, then we'll see about food," Matthew said as he wrapped an arm around my shoulders and led me into a large wood beamed living room full of stuffed chairs and comfortable sofas. You can only imagine, or maybe you can't, my surprise to find Leopold

LEOPOLD CHRIST

Christ sitting on one of those comfortable sofas.

I came to a stop and Matthew saw the look on my face.

"I believe you two know each other," he said playfully. "In fact, Leo and I were just talking about you."

"And what was it you were talking about?" I asked as I moved to sit in a chair beyond the sofas that faced each other.

"Danny, grab a seat on one of the sofas will you please," Matt said. "I like to sit in that chair. It's a little harder than the others and easier on my back." I veered off and settled onto the sofa across from Leopold Christ.

"You look well rested, my dear friend," Leopold said. "I was very concerned about you when we last spoke. You looked quite exhausted after your Brazil trip."

"I am feeling great, Leo. Just great. Why are you here?"

"What did I tell you, Mr. President," Leo said with a smile. "With him, there is never any small talk. Always, right to the point." Then he looked at me. "I have been talking with your brother for an hour now, Daniel. A very nice conversation. Two men speaking of things that have very little importance, except when we were talking about

238

you, of course, and we felt no urgency of getting to the point. And your brother is the busiest man in the world. There is much you could learn from him."

I looked at Matthew. "Why is he here?"

Matthew smiled at me. "Mr. Christ called and suggested the three of us should get together and discuss your discoveries. He has led me to believe they are momentous."

"And after our discussion over dinner last week, I didn't convince you that Leopold Christ may be harboring ulterior motives?"

"Mr. Christ is a generous donor to our campaign. I see no harm in having a conversation, Danny. In fact, I find Mr. Christ to be quite informed."

I took a visual tour of the room while I composed myself. I suppose it isn't so bad that Leo is here. Maybe, in the presence of the President, Leopold Christ will finally reveal what it was he wanted. His end game. I would keep my temper, attempt to get Leo to say to Matthew what he had said to me, and allow Matthew to see that we were in the company of a seriously delusional old man.

"What can I get everyone?" Matthew asked.

LEOPOLD CHRIST

I asked for a cold beer. Mark and Leo asked for iced tea. When we all had our drinks and were comfortable, Matthew said, "Leo, Danny has told me about the two digs. Described them quite vividly, I must say. They sounded extraordinary. And quite important, I would think. He also told me a little about you. What he told me was also quite extraordinary. I think I would like to hear your story from you, if that is alright?"

"It is why I am here, Mr. President," Leo said. "And I don't mean here in this cabin. Allow me to begin at the beginning, if I may, sir. Interrupt any time you have a question, or confusion about something. It is vitally important that you understand it all."

"And why is that, Leo?" Matthew asked.

Leaning back into the cushions and placing his iced tea on the side table, Leo said, "Mr. President, I will get to that. But first, if I may, allow me to tell my story."

Matthew leaned back in his chair and opened his arms. "Mr. Christ, I am all ears."

Leo actually began the story at the beginning of recorded time from his world, not from the discovery of a dying sun. He spoke of the constant warring that tribes of his world fought over thousands of years, eventually forming three great powers through countless alliances. He worked his way to a dying sun, the asteroid collision, the realization that their world was on borrowed time. Matthew listened without interruption, occasionally looking over at me. I sat passively, made no comment or physical display of any sort. I would let Leopold Christ have his say. I would have mine when he finished.

"When the entire scientific community proclaimed the planet was now living on borrowed time, that had a very sobering effect," Leopold said. "It took a while for the enormity of the situation to sink in, several generations, in fact, but reality does have a way of slapping some sense into people, don't you think, Mr. President?"

"That has been my experience," Matthew said with a smile. "Everyone has a Plan A. The smart ones also have a Plan B. And the cautious a Plan C. The pages of our history books are filled with people and countries that had great ambitions. Some who even realized those ambitions. But they couldn't sustain them. No Plan B.

"I have often wondered," Matthew continued, as he went and got more iced tea, "what it might take for the governments of Earth to act as one. Could we all agree on a course of action if, let's say, our planet was faced with a deadly pandemic of biblical proportions? Would we unite to ward off an ecological disaster that could alter life on the planet?

"Sad to say," said Matthew as he sat back down, "things like that have not united us yet. But, what if the threat came from beyond our world? You say that happened on your planet, Leo."

"Yes, sir, it did. But we did not come together right away. There were hundreds of years of discussions between the three nations with no progress and all the while science was sounding an alarm. Generations passed. And then one man made unification his life's objective and he did it."

"Tell me about this man," Matthew said. "What do the history books say about him?"

Leo sat silent for a few seconds, looking across the room toward the windows and the trees beyond. When he looked at my brother, his eyes had that intensity that I had first seen in my office barely six months ago that now seemed like six years.

"I believe some men are born to greatness," Leo said. "Would you agree with that statement, sir?"

Matthew smiled. "I wouldn't disagree with it. But I do think men are the masters of their fate."

"Yes," Leo replied, "but most men's fate is not greatness. Most men lack many of the qualities that are required."

"I can't agree with you there, Mr. Christ," Mark said crossing one knee over the other. "Our history books are full of the names of men, and women, who came from nothing and rose to greatness."

"Very true, Mr. Sharpe," Leo said, "but there are many more names of men and women who fell far short of expectations. More infamy than fame. And that is because they were lacking. Perhaps they lacked a credible opportunity. Perhaps they fell short in the quality of empathy, or the intellectual capacity to actually make a difference. Maybe, they lacked vision and found the opportunity for bad far outweighed the benefits of good."

Leo sipped his tea and arched his eyebrows, and then said,

"For every Joan of Arc there a thousand Marie Antoinette's. For every Gandhi a thousand Henry the Eighths." He looked at me then and asked, "What about you, my young friend? Do you believe all men can attain greatness?"

The question caught me off guard. I had had no intention of saying anything until Leo was done with his story. I noticed my brother was looking at me with a look of humor in his eyes. This was the sort of question our father would pose at the dinner table when I was in high school and Matthew was home from university. Invariably, my answer to whatever the question posed would lead to a sad shake of the old man's head and a failed suppression of a smile from Matthew.

I shrugged. "I agree with the President. I believe men are the masters of their fate. I just happen to think most men make poor choices. And we would need more than a few days to discuss the reasons for that. Why don't we stick to your story, Leo. Curb your fondness for going off on tangents."

Leo smiled. "You see, Mr. President. This is why your brother has attained greatness. He sees an objective clearly

244

and moves relentlessly toward it."

"I found some bones," I said, with perhaps a tinge of frustration. "There was no greatness in it. Just a discovery of bones."

"Not just a discovery," Leo said. "The greatest discovery."

I looked at Matthew and he had a huge grin on his face. "Could we please get on with it?" I sighed.

"Tell me about the man who united your world, Leo," Matthew said with a smile. "We can save the discussion of how men become great for another time."

With a slight bow of his head, Leo said, "He was born in the West to a daughter of the ruling family at the time. By the time the boy grew into a man, he had attended the finest schools, and had learned about war, governing, intrigue, politics, by sitting at the knee of his grandfather, the leader of the nation. The grandfather was preparing him so he could eventually conquer the East and the North when he rose to the leadership position on the old man's death. But the boy knew that war would never unify the world, although he never shared those thoughts with his grandfather. He was

245

very concerned with the inevitable fate of the rock planet even though his grandfather said that fifty thousand years was a long time and should be of no concern to them now. And then one day an opportunity presented itself."

Leo looked at the three of us one at a time. "It was an opportunity for greatness, if he chose to pursue it. And pursue it he did. When the man was thirty years old, the grandfather died. A year later, his mother lay on her death bed. She called him to her side and gave him a hand written letter she had composed. Hand written letters were almost extinct by this time. Technology had advanced to the point where writing implements were quite passe. And then she told him who his true father was. It was not the man he thought it was who had died when he was eight. His biological father was now the leader of the North. The young mother and future leader had had a tryst during a diplomatic visit. She had never told her mate, who died believing he was the father. She had never told her father, fearing he would be furious and probably banish them into exile. She never told the man who fathered him. The letter she gave her son would do that, if he decided to make the truth known to his counterpart in the North. Which, of course, he did. The reports I have read all say the same thing. The leader of the North did not need to read the letter from his long ago lover. He had taken one look at the young man and knew he was his son. The resemblance left no doubt. It took some years for the young leader to then forge an alliance with the East, but the East knew they would be no match militarily against the combined strength of the other two nations. Before the man died at a very old age, he had floated the idea of a ruling council, and the planet is still ruled by a council to this day."

"So that is how your world came to be ruled by a council," said Matthew. "But what of the man? Do your history accounts speak of the man himself?"

Leo looked at my brother and there was a softening of his gaze, a whisper to his voice. "By all accounts I have read, sir, he was a man of great courage. A man of unimpeachable character. A man who suffered some difficult personal tragedies, yet overcame them. He was a selfless man. I believe on this planet you call men such as he, saints. You can only imagine, sir, the difficult task he had set for himself trying to unite a world that had been at war for forty

247

thousand years. His powers of persuasion must have been immense. But his character must have been above reproach for mortal enemies to agree to his pleas." Then Leo smiled. "And that is why I say, some men are born to greatness. It was a moment in time when something monumental was attainable, and here was the one man who could attain it."

Matthew nodded. "I get your point, Leo. When a man attains a position of power, like I have as President, there is an almost overwhelming desire to do something really meaningful. Something profound that will resonate through the years. Often, that doesn't happen. Obstacles are in the way or the dream is short-sighted."

"Or the man is not capable enough to pull it off," Leo said.

"Or he is not capable enough to pull it off," Matthew agreed. "It takes a great deal of stamina to swim against the tide. A great deal of courage, too."

"But of course it does, Mr. President," said Leo. "If it was easy, everyone would be great."

Then my brother looked at Leopold Christ and I recognized that look on his face. He was probing for

248

information without asking a direct question. Matthew was very good at that.

"So your world united against the threat from the unstable planet, is that right, Leo?"

Leo nodded.

"I have wondered," Matthew said, "if the nations of Earth would unite as one if the threat came from space. Would that be the one thing that could actually unite the world? An alliance to save mankind, whether from the threat of an asteroid or the aggression of an alien race. Is that what it would take?"

Leo smiled that grotesque smile and said, "Well, if the entertaining movies I have watched are any indication, my dear Mr. President, Earth will vanquish all aggressors. And they will do so as one united entity." Then the smile faded slightly. "But that is Hollywood. Always the happy ending."

"You don't like happy endings, Mr. Christ?" Mark asked.

"Oh, I do, sir, I do. It's just that in that situation the described happy ending is Plan A. I would advise having a Plan B and C. In reality, believing that Earth could defeat any threat from an invading alien race would be folly."

249

"And why is that?" Mark asked.

Leo shifted his gaze to the Chief of Staff. "Quite simple, Mr. Sharpe. Any alien race that has the technology to get here with a threatening force, will have the technology to destroy any aggression this planet can summon against them. That is reality."

I looked at my brother. He was looking out the windows and I could tell he was deep in thought. Then he turned his attention back to Leopold Christ.

"So what happened next?" Matthew asked.

∧   ∧

Leopold spoke of technological advances and the early years of space exploration. The exploration of galaxies that led to the discovery that Earth could be a destination for survivors of a doomed planet. He spoke of the changing dynamics of his world and the successful mining of another world that was slowly spinning into oblivion. And when he spoke of the creation of the warriors, he did so with the same reverence I had witnessed earlier.

"So these warriors were sent to Earth," Matthew said, "and these are the bones Danny discovered?"

"Correct," said Leo.

"Twelve thousand years ago?"

"Correct again, sir."

"And they were sent here to do battle with the men of Earth. Is that also correct?"

Leo nodded.

"Now, I know I am not the smartest guy in the room when it comes to prehistoric times," Matthew said, looking over at me, "but even I know there was no civilization to speak of. Who did they come here to fight? What, exactly, was their objective? Couldn't have been just mindless killing. As you said earlier, Leo, any race capable of flying to distant planets would have an easy time of defeating another race who had not advanced that far. What threat could cavemen possibly present and why bother to come here thousands of years before they actually had to?"

"Doctor Reynolds posed the same question to me when I told him why the warriors had been sent to Earth," Leo said. Then he looked at me. "Do you recall my answer, Daniel?"

"Of course," I said.

"And what was the reason?" Mark asked. "I agree with

251

the President. Why come to do battle thousands of years before a fight for dominance of the planet was actually needed."

Leo looked at me and gave a slight nod. I frowned.

"Mr. Christ," I said, "said the warriors were sent here to eradicate the homo sapiens known as Neanderthal."

"And why was that?" asked Mark.

"Because," I said, folding my arms across my chest, "Neanderthal aggression against Cro Magnon was limiting advancement by Cro Magnon. If Earth was to make any progress toward being a civilized planet, the brutish Neanderthal would have to be eliminated."

"I'm sorry," Mark said, leaning back into the cushions. "I am having a hard time buying all of this, Mr. Christ. Why come to fight battles to destroy an entire species thousands of years before it would be necessary? It makes no sense."

"Dominant countries do it all the time, Mr. Sharpe," Leo said. "They have been doing it throughout the history of Earth. A squabble begins in a third world country and the super powers take sides. No? Even your administration, and the previous two, have had to make choices on who to

252

support. Weapons, technology and often human support are sent into the battle. No difference."

"Except we are not waging a war of genocide," Mark said.

"But others have," said Leo.

"Mr. Christ," Matthew said, interrupting his Chief of Staff who was about to say something, "I think it is time you told us about the first people to come to Earth from your planet."

I looked at my brother. I couldn't tell if he was buying into this nonsense or still trying to trip up Leopold Christ. I said nothing, and had no idea where this was heading now, but Matthew had certainly piqued my interest.

"Yes," said Leo, "I suppose it is." Then he looked at me. "I thought, perhaps, my young friend would have posed that question several weeks ago, but he did not. His reluctance to accept the evidence before him prevented that question from being asked. And, frankly, Daniel's concern has always been about the bones. Always the bones. Never the reason for the bones being here."

"Well, now I am asking," the President said.

Leo nodded. "When it was determined that Earth was to be the planet that would harbor the people of my doomed planet, it was also determined that those who would be fleeing here in the distant future would not be fleeing to an uncivilized world, populated by brutish men of low intelligence. Earth needed to be prepared to accept an advanced civilization. Of course, there was no great urgency exhibited by the council, but plans were discussed and then implemented."

Leo looked at my brother. Matthew said, "Continue."

"Forty thousand years ago, one thousand babies grew to adulthood in the grasslands and caves of a desolate section of my planet. They survived off whatever the land and the wild life could provide. The adults that were there were not their parents. Neither were they there to teach. They were tasked with simply nurturing the children into early adulthood and having the children observe the means by which to survive. There were no modern conveniences. In fact, there were no conveniences at all. As far as the children knew, this was how life was lived and there were no other people in existence except them.

"During the twenty odd years that they lived there, the council had ships built that would take them to Earth. When the time came, the entire group was gassed into unconsciousness, placed into a coma, and almost three years later were deposited in the lower extremities of the land mass now called Africa, below the receding ice. This was done three times in succeeding generations. Three groups of one thousand young males and females, placed here to populate this planet, to build a civilization, to prepare this world for the arrival of their species."

"Ridiculous," I said.

"So, you are saying that modern man, us, are actually descendants of people from your planet," said Matthew.

Leo nodded. "We are one and the same, Mr. President. The bones your brother has discovered, of the warriors from my planet, prove that without any doubt. Is that not true, Daniel?"

Matt looked at me. "Matthew, this is crazy," I said. "The DNA is the same as ours, yes. But that doesn't mean they came from some other planet. It doesn't preclude them from being Earthlings. If anything, it proves they are from

Earth."

"Because the DNA is the same?" Matt said.

"Yes," I replied.

"Which means," Matt said, "if the warriors did come from another planet, then so did our ancestors."

fifteen

I am sure my sigh was probably louder and more dramatic than should have been exhibited, but my frustration is immense right now.

"Mr. President," I said softly, measuring each word I was about to say, "in hundreds of years of documented digs, by the most respected names in archaeology, there has never been any evidence found that would support any argument that extra-terrestrials visited this world, let alone populated it. Modern man was the next evolutionary step in the long chain that brought us here. Everything we know points to that."

257

Matthew looked at Leo. "I'm sure this isn't going exactly as you expected, is it Mr. Christ?"

"No, sir, it is not," Leo said with a shake of the head. "My concern, all along, was that you would have doubts about what I must tell you about buried bones when I came to you with the man who unearthed them. You would question me, you would question the archaeologist, you would question the validity of the find. And rightly so. Imagine the relief I felt when the archaeologist who found the bones was your brother. The one man out of eight billion people you would trust implicitly. Sending Daniel on the second dig was too validate everything, leaving no doubt in his mind, thus leaving no doubt in yours. But he refuses to be swayed."

"Because I have never seen documentation of extra-terrestrial visitation," I said forcefully, leaning forward on the sofa.

"But I have," Matthew calmly said to me. After a brief pause allowing that to sink in, he said, "And I will deny saying that."

I was stunned. My brother saw that, smiled at me and gave a slight nod. And I believed him.

258

"So," Matthew said, looking back at Leo, "tell me again about these warriors."

While Leo speaks of the killers who destroyed the Neanderthal, I am having all kinds of thoughts going through my head, and that feeling of unease surrounds me again. I begin replaying the conversations I had had with Leo, going back to that first day in my office. I was missing something. Something, I am sure, that is important.

"So the warriors do their job, with a glitch here or there," Matthew said, "and their children do their job. Then what?"

"Nothing," said Leo. "There is no recorded history that anything else was done for a very long time. It appears all the councils going forward thought it best to just allow time to do what time does best. Years pass. The population grows. Progress is made."

"Yet, you are here, Mr. Christ."

"Yes."

"And you are not the first."

"No, sir, I am not."

"Tell me."

Leopold Christ then told my brother of the men, who

over thousands of years, had been sent to Earth to try to aid in pushing along the progress of man."

"So, from the earliest moments of recorded time, there has been a presence here to help spur us along," Matthew said.

"In all honesty, Mr. President, no one really knows how much influence these men actually had in the history of this world," said Leo. "I have read the reports that were sent back, chronicling leaps forward in progress, and boasting of their influence in that progress. But who is to really say? In reality, there have been thousands of years when nothing of any substance was accomplished by those sent here. Again, like the rogue warriors, some men can be unreliable agents when left to their own devices. Not like a trained dog or a coded robot. In fact, Mr. President, I could tell you stories of some who came and almost immediately began nefarious deeds.

"Overall, I suspect these visits did help man move forward, but I had the feeling when I was reading the accounts, that most councils really were not that concerned. There were still thousands of years before Armageddon, and

260

once cities began to be erected here it was known that progress would happen. It was just a matter of time, and time was on our side."

Sandwiches, snacks and drinks were brought into the room and set on several small tables. We got what we wanted and went back to our seats. I hadn't said anything in quite a while and as Matthew handed me a beer he asked if I was alright. I said I was fine. And then he asked where I thought this was all heading to. I shrugged and said nothing. But I had a feeling that I knew.

"Let me ask you something, Mr. Christ," Matthew said, settling in his chair once again. "Do you know of other civilizations who inhabit the universe?"

"As far as I know there are none, although I suspect there probably are," Leo said. "If any were discovered after I left, I would not know about them." Then Leo smiled. "Of course, Mr. President, I would not have been privy to that information. It would have had nothing to do with my assignment."

"But you think there may be?"

"I have no idea, sir. We knew there were four planets

discovered that had a breathable atmosphere where we could survive. And some water. Two of them had vegetation and things that crawled. As far as I knew, none had anything more intelligent than a spider. The last such planet was discovered four thousand years ago. It is my belief that the councils over the years had some curiosity about life elsewhere, but tremendous resources and wealth have been dedicated to the time when we would need to leave and come here, so resources for further exploration were limited."

Matthew digested that tidbit while he chewed a turkey sandwich. "We believe Earth has been visited over the years and that visitation activity may have substantially increased in the last sixty years," he said. "Would you know anything about that?"

Leo was nibbling on some lettuce he had pulled from his sandwich. He gazed at my brother for a long time before he spoke. "People like myself have been coming here for a long time, like I said. We have not been the only ones."

"Elaborate, please," Matthew said, placing his sandwich on a table and leaning forward in his chair with a grimace as a back spasm shook him.

"As I told my young friend, Daniel, no one who ever set foot on Earth has gone back to their home planet. We could not risk the devastation of another pandemic. However, that did not stop periodic observations of Earth and the monitoring of conditions here, giving the councils a clearer understanding of progress.

"Several thousand years ago, when the time to reach Earth from Eden had been almost halved, larger ships came here with scientists and doctors on board prepared to perform experiments on everything from rocks to soil to flora and fauna. Especially humans."

"But according to you, humans are you," Mark Sharpe said. "What mysteries were they hoping to find?"

"Diseases, of course, were the main concern, Mr. Sharpe," Christ said. "And they certainly discovered an abundance of them. And, of course, different regions had their own particular pathogens, so it was not an easy task. Obviously, we would need to find anti-bodies and serums to inoculate every person who would be taking the final voyage to Earth, in order to insure their survival."

"What does that mean, 'every person taking the final

263

voyage'?" asked Mark.

"Obviously," I said, "not everyone is going to survive the cataclysm. Isn't that so, Leo?"

Leopold Christ shrugged. "There are currently five billion people on my home planet. Do the math, sir. Even if ships were built that could carry ten thousand people, one thousand such crafts would only bring ten million people to Earth. Perhaps there are two thousand such vessels, but I would be surprised if there were that many."

"So, is the plan to shuttle to Earth ten million people at a time when the time comes?" Mark asked. "And how does Earth accommodate five billion more people? We are already bursting at the seams."

Leo shrugged again. "As Doctor Reynolds has said, not everyone will survive the destruction."

"Only the best and the brightest," Matthew whispered across the silence. "And the wealthiest. Have to have room for the rich." Then he looked at Mark. "Not much different than our doomsday plan, is it? It just sounds more disgusting when actually said out loud."

Matt said, "Tell me more about these monitoring

flights."

"I'm afraid, Mr. President, that you may find some of what I can tell you quite disturbing."

"Mr. Christ, there has been nothing that you have told me that I have not already found quite disturbing. Might as well hear it all."

"As I have mentioned," Leo said, "The early monitoring was to keep tabs on progress. Those flights let the council know that Neanderthal were a problem, thus the arrival of the warriors. Later flights provided more information and guided decisions going forward, which led to people like myself being sent here. Several thousand years ago, about the time of the Roman dominance, the crafts coming to Earth were larger and carried scientists and doctors. Under extremely stringent bio-hazard conditions, fauna and flora of Earth were probed and dissected. From the fly to the orca and everything in between. Every kind of flower that bloomed, every tree, plant, bush. Fruits, vegetables. Soils, rocks, life on reefs. Everything. Including humans.

"During one of the earlier flights, a DNA test of one of

the humans showed a disparity that was quite disturbing. It showed an influence of Neanderthal DNA in the make-up. A future flight had a DNA sample that showed what proved to be Denisovan influence. These tests caused great concern among members of the council. It was thought our bloodline here on Earth was pure and would remain so until we came."

"So, no one had given any thought to the possibility that in twenty-five thousand years of co-habitation on the planet, the two species would not have hooked up?" Mark Sharpe said, and then he laughed. "How the hell did you guys ever get a craft off the ground, let alone all the way to Earth?"

Leo frowned. "I have no idea what their thought process was back then. It seems that no one considered it. I can only speculate why, but the reality is they didn't expect it."

"And this was a problem?" asked Matthew.

"It was to the people on the council back then," answered Leo. "Frankly, sir, it is to this council, also. And to every council in between. The bloodlines on my planet are pure."

Matthew pursed his lips. "Continue, Mr. Christ."

"More flights were sent to Earth. More probing into

266

desolate sections of the planet, which, obviously, at the time was most of the land mass. If it appeared there was an influence of another species in the DNA of that particular village or tribe, the entire populace was exterminated."

"You cannot be serious," Mark said, leaning forward in his chair.

"Did this happen often, Mr. Christ?" Matthew calmly asked.

"I have read many accounts of such action, Mr. President. I'm sure there were many others that were unreported and just done as SOP."

"Your people seem to have no value of human life," Matthew said. "No value at all."

"I would not dispute that statement, sir," Leo said softly. "I certainly do not condone these actions. They sicken me. As I have told your brother, I have been on Earth for a very long time now and consider myself a citizen of this planet and not the one I came from."

"Obviously, the extermination of Earth man has ceased," said Matthew. "We have no reports of entire communities disappearing."

"The practice continues to this day," said Leo. "Very remote tribes. More populated areas will be dealt with when the time comes."

"What the hell does that mean!" Mark said, his voice rising.

"Exactly what it sounds like," I said. "Many tribes and civilizations have ceased to exist since prehistoric times. Often, we have no idea why. We have attributed their demise to famine, disease, butchery by conquering armies, a destructive act of Nature. It is still happening today. In the jungles along the equator. In the deserts and mountains. In the cold of Siberia and Tibet."

"Okay," Mark said, "but he's saying people of Earth will be, what, tracked down and killed? Is that what you are saying, Mr. Christ, when the space ships start landing in some future time? What percentage of humans carry Neanderthal and, what was the other one, Denisovan, blood? Does anyone know?"

"Roughly five percent," said Leo. "Obviously, that number would have been higher were it not for the actions taken over the years."

268

"You are talking about the extermination of four hundred million people," Matthew said, "at current population levels. How much that number grows in the time left before they come is anyone's guess. Could this council actually believe that the people of Earth would stand by and allow that to happen?"

"We've discussed this already, Mr. President," said Leo. "There will be nothing you can do to prevent it."

A million thoughts were bouncing around in my mind. "If you insist on believing this tale from Leopold Christ," I said to my brother, "then you can believe him when he tells you Earth would be defenseless against an attack. Certainly, the Earth of today.

"I have been sitting here thinking, Matthew. And one of the problems I have had with Leo's story is, why aren't we a more advanced civilization than we currently are? Why has it taken forty thousand years for us to get where we are, if there was a far more intelligent civilization looking over our shoulder? Why didn't they teach us electricity ten thousand years ago? Why did we not create things in factories eight thousand years ago? Why were we still riding buckboards a

269

hundred and twenty years ago?"

I looked at Leo and answered my question. "Because then we would have developed too fast. We may have matched the technology of those who spied upon us. We may have even developed weapons that could protect Earth from unwanted visitors, even if they are distant cousins."

Leo smiled. "You see, Mr. President, why your brother is so necessary a piece to all of this. Had I brought another scientist to this meeting, you may have thought that to be a rehearsed response to this discussion. But from the mouth of Daniel, you know it is not. And he is correct. The councils have wanted Earth to be sufficiently accommodating, but still technologically inferior."

"Let me ask you something," I said to Leo. "You have made a big deal several times now about this magnificent man who united your world. His powers of persuasion. Doing something no one else could have done. Do you look at my brother as being the same kind of man? Is it your intention to convince President Reynolds that he must meet with the world leaders? That he must convince them of the impending arrival of visitors from outer space arriving in the

270

next few thousand years? Is it your hope that he can rally the entire community of Earth so they can prepare themselves? From day one, I have tried to figure out your end game. Is this it?"

Leo sat passively on the sofa, legs crossed, hands folded in his lap, looking small and ancient. When he spoke, his voice was soft. "Mr. President," Leo said, looking at my brother, "I watched you from the very beginning of the primary process, as I did all the others who hoped to be elected to President. I saw in you, someone who I believed had a great integrity. Sincerity came through in every speech you made. People believed you. And not because they wanted to because you were telling them what they wanted to hear, but because they believed you were promising them a better future. You were giving them hope and they believed you. Through your words and past actions, you rallied an electorate to stand with you. Early on, I recognized that power of persuasion that you have, which is why you had my financial support. My dear friend, Daniel, is correct. Those powers of persuasion will be needed."

Then Leopold Christ, barely above a whisper, said, "I

am afraid I have failed in my assignment, Mr. President, and that places a terrible burden on you. I truly am sorry."

Matthew looked over at me, obviously confused by what Leo had just said, and wondering if I have a clue what the old man is talking about. I do not, although the feeling of doom is again creeping up my back.

"You'll have to explain yourself, Mr. Christ," the President said. "How have you failed? What are you talking about?"

"Those of us who have been sent to Earth have come with simple directions," Leo said, "especially the last few of us. As I have said, we were to encourage progress when we could. An effort to make Earth a more advanced society. But we were also tasked with the directive to do our best to retard advancement in offensive weaponry and space travel, should the planet ever make sufficient advances in that direction." Leo shrugged. "I couldn't stop the space programs of Russia and the United States. I didn't have that kind of influence. But infrequent sojourns to the moon are hardly reasons for concern, and little has been done in the last sixty years. So, I have had some success there."

272

He leaned back into the cushions and sighed. "My failure, I'm afraid, is weaponry. Leading up to, and during your first World War, I was here in America, strengthening my dealings with some of the great men who powered the growth of the world during the early decades of the twentieth century. When the economic crash came, I went back to Europe. For me, it was a time of reflection and rest. And observation. Early on, I saw what Hitler could accomplish in Germany and I understood what his intentions were. Even before he advanced into Poland, I had heard the whispers about the scientists who labored to solve the mysteries that would allow the building of super weapons. Rockets to blaze across the sky. Bombs that could level cities. The technology they searched for, was, of course, primitive to the scientists of my planet, but I knew what such weapons could mean on this planet."

Leo smiled and his eyebrows raised. "Through a great deal of persuasion on my part, and also a great deal of money, some scientists were persuaded to leave Germany before the Nazi's marched into Paris. They were spirited away to America, much to the chagrin of an enraged Hitler.

273

So, I managed to keep Nazi Germany from producing an atomic bomb. Unfortunately, I could not do the same for the Manhattan Project."

It hit me then. I should have picked up on it sooner. Should have understood what Leo had been telling me all this time. And maybe I would have, had I not been so sure there was some nefarious intent behind it all.

"So we have you to thank for winning the war?" Mark said. "Mr. President, I think we have heard enough. I think your brother is correct. None of this is remotely believable."

I looked at Leo and smiled. "Leo, please finish your story and tell the President what you require of him. It is time." Looking over at Matthew, I saw that he, too, understood. The look from Leo was unmistakable as he realized I finally knew what this was all about.

"August 6th and August 9th, 1945," Leo said. "When I reported back to the council what had transpired on those dates, I received numerous communiques demanding to know more. That Earth stepping into the nuclear age caused a great deal of anxiety in the council. Over the last eighty years, I have tried to decipher the mixed messages I have received. The demands are always the same, however. What progress is being made here on Earth regarding nuclear weapons? I have kept them apprised. The proliferation by the super powers, detente, and now the arsenals kept by lesser powers. It is that which most concerns the council. The three super powers of my world all held weapons that could destroy the planet while they waged war on each other forty thousand years ago. But to use them would have been madness. So there was concern when the super powers of Earth tamed the atom, but it was a reasoned concern. The concern that lesser nations have this power is not as reasonable."

"Several times," I said to Matthew, "when I have expressed doubts about alien bones and visitors from other worlds, Leo would say to me, 'if there were time, how many warriors would we need to dig up to convince you'. I always assumed we didn't have time to do that because Leo was very old and didn't have much more time to live. I was wrong."

Matthew nodded. "How much time do we have, Mr. Christ?"

"I don't know, sir," Leo said. "But they are on their

way. The increased activity your air force has noticed confirms that. But there could be two reasons for that increase.

"Explain," said Matthew tersely.

"These could be advance flights that are selecting places where the migration crafts could land," Leo said, and then hesitated.

"Or?" said Matthew.

"Or they could be reconnoitering for a military presence that will destroy all weapons of mass destruction here on Earth. Their lasers would destroy all silos, all submarines carrying nuclear missiles, any facility that is used to make weapon grade material." Leopold Christ leaned forward on the sofa. "Believe me when I tell you, sir, they would have no problem accomplishing that feat."

Matthew stared at Christ for many moments and raised a hand as Mark was about to say something.

"You don't know what is coming. Only that something is. Could be military, could be civilian." said the President.

"I have not been told anything," Mr. President. "But they are coming. I am sure of it. I have sent missives and

276

received no answers. They are coming."

"What is your best guess, Mr. Christ?" asked the President.

"It was my understanding before I came to Earth, that my world may have had another thousand years before exodus would be required. But if the rock planet has become completely unstable that prediction would prove untenable. Now, with the threat of nuclear weapons in the hands of many, and an uninhabitable world that such weapons could create, the council may have been spurred into doing the only thing they could do."

"Of course," Matthew said. "And you want me to tell the world what you have just told me."

"You must tell them, sir. You must convince them that resistance would be foolish. You must convince the world leaders that they come in peace and that they truly are your brothers."

"Except for the half a billion who aren't," Matthew said.

"Yes. Except for them," said Leopold Christ.

"And will this council now expect that they will rule

this world?" Mark angrily asked.

None of us bothered to answer. There was no need.

THE END